KU-507-000

"When Were You Going To Tell Me, Scarlett?"

"Tell you what?"

"That you're pregnant."

If Raiden had told her he was an alien, then flew around the room to prove it, she wouldn't have been more stunned.

Slowly, carefully, as if testing her voice for the first time, she said, "Never, I guess. Since I'm not."

His eyes suddenly took on a faraway look. "I *have* been feeling it in every inch of you. But I didn't reach the obvious conclusion because I thought you'd tell me if it was true. But you didn't." His eyes focused on hers again, something enormous roiling in their depths. "Why, Scarlett? Was it because you thought we'd say goodbye and I didn't have to know?"

Scandalously Expecting His Child

OLIVIA GATES

All rights reserved including the right of reproduction
in whole or in part in any form. This edition is published
by arrangement with Harlequin Books S.A.

This is a work of fiction. Names, characters, places,
locations and incidents are purely fictional and bear no
relationship to any real life individuals, living or dead, or
to any actual places, business establishments, locations,
events or incidents. Any resemblance is entirely
coincidental.

This book is sold subject to the condition that it shall
not, by way of trade or otherwise, be lent, resold, hired
out or otherwise circulated without the prior consent
of the publisher in any form of binding or cover other
than that in which it is published and without a similar
condition including this condition being imposed on the
subsequent purchaser.

® and TM are trademarks owned and used by the
trademark owner and/or its licensee. Trademarks
marked with ® are registered with the United Kingdom
Patent Office and/or the Office for Harmonisation in the
Internal Market and in other countries.

First published in Great Britain 2014
by Mills & Boon, an imprint of Harlequin (UK) Limited,
Large Print edition 2015
Eton House, 18-24 Paradise Road,
Richmond, Surrey, TW9 1SR

© 2014 Olivia Gates

ISBN: 978-0-263-25981-0

Harlequin (UK) Limited's policy is to use papers that
are natural, renewable and recyclable products and made
from wood grown in sustainable forests. The logging
and manufacturing processes conform to the legal
environmental regulations of the country of origin.

Printed and bound in Great Britain
by CPI Antony Rowe, Chippenham, Wiltshire

OLIVIA GATES

has always pursued creative passions such as singing and handicrafts. She still does, but only one of her passions grew gratifying enough, consuming enough, to become an ongoing career—writing.

She is most fulfilled when she is creating worlds and conflicts for her characters, then exploring and untangling them bit by bit, sharing her protagonists' every heart-wrenching heartache and hope, their every heart-pounding doubt and trial, until she leads them to an indisputably earned and gloriously satisfying happy ending.

When she's not writing, she is a doctor, a wife to her own alpha male and a mother to one brilliant girl and one demanding Angora cat. Visit Olivia at www.oliviagates.com

ROTHERHAM LIBRARY & INFORMATION SERVICES

F

B52032617X

To Stacy Boyd, my incredible editor, who's supported me throughout the toughest two years of my life.

One

Raiden Kuroshiro looked down at the woman standing beside him. Megumi was indeed her name. A beautiful blessing. With flawless white skin, gleaming raven hair and naturally red lips, she looked like a real live version of Snow White. And with her small, svelte body wrapped to perfection in that vivid blue dress, she did look like a fairy-tale princess. There was something regal about her bearing as she received everyone's congratulations on their engagement. Their wedding was exactly ten weeks from tonight.

And he felt absolutely nothing for her.

Thankfully, her feelings for him were as non-existent.

Which was as it should be.

The reasons he was marrying Megumi, and the ones she had to marry him, didn't necessitate they even tolerated each other. Theirs would be a pure marriage of convenience.

Megumi looked up at him, ultrapoliteness playing on her dainty lips. Though smiling wasn't one of his usual activities, it was easy to answer her smile. Not that he had anything to do with it. Known as an angel, Megumi would get along with the devil himself. Which she did. Raiden was known as a fiend. He'd been called that during his years as a mercenary, and worse as he'd slashed his way to the top of the venture capitalism field and carved himself a permanent place there.

"I can join my mother if you like."

He barely heard Megumi over the traditional *gagaku* court music and the loud drone of the five hundred people filling the ballroom. It was the first time he'd been with that many members of Japanese society's upper crust in one place. It was his goal not only to belong to that class but to rule it. Megumi knew that, and she was thoughtfully offering to slip away so he could make the most of the event without her hindering presence.

Though it was a tempting offer, he shook his head. He was under said upper crust's microscope, and he knew it would be frowned upon to leave his bride-to-be in their first public appearance together, especially one dedicated to celebrating their impending union.

But at least he didn't have to play the besotted groom, as he would have had to in Western societies. It was a relief that in Japanese society prospective partners in traditionally arranged marriages demonstrated nothing more than utmost courtesy to each other. Which was easy with Megumi. He didn't have to feign gallantry with her.

Not that he liked her. He didn't like anyone. Apart from his Black Castle "brothers"—who were integral parts of his own being—he categorized people in limited roles. He had allies, subordinates and enemies. Megumi fell somewhere between the first two categories. He'd made her position in his life clear, and she seemed accepting of it.

Which she should. He was the wealthiest, most powerful husband and future father of her children she could have. Even if he weren't already the ultimate catch, as an obedient daughter, Megumi would have still married him. Her father wanted Raiden as family at any cost.

And *that* was the main reason he was marrying her. She was his only path to the one thing he'd dreamed of all his life, what he'd been working to achieve for the past ten years.

Reclaiming his birthright.

But though everything was going according to plan, one thing niggled at him. The other reason he was marrying Megumi was to have full-blooded Japanese heirs. Which meant he would have to...perform. He worried he wouldn't be able to. Not without falling back on what managed to thaw his deep-frozen libido. Fantasizing about *her.*

It was galling he'd have to resort to this measure to...rise to the occasion, but he was brutally pragmatic. He'd resort to whatever worked.

Hopefully only once. With careful timing, it might be all it took to impregnate Megumi.

After conception, it was another major relief that most Japanese wives in arranged marriages mostly retreated to their own quarters, with their lives from then on revolving around their baby. From what he'd been hearing about the society that was still alien to him, in the kind of marriage he was entering, it was accepted that a husband's role was as a sperm donor and financier. His wife mostly relegated him to public social activities and appearances, with his intimacy sought again only when another baby was needed. Which was exactly the kind of marriage he wanted. The only kind he could stomach.

He looked at Megumi as she graciously smiled at another congratulator and wondered at his intense aversion to the idea of sex with her. If anyone knew he thought having sex with such a beauty was such a terrible fate, they'd question his virility. If they knew he'd have to invoke another woman's memory to go through with it, they'd think him pathetic. If they knew that woman had been a fraud, they'd question his judgment. But if they knew that not even finding out the truth about her had lessened her hold over him, it would totally decimate the uncompromising identity he presented to the world.

Not that anyone would ever learn of her. Or of any of his other dark secrets. He'd accumulated unspeakable ones during the twenty years when he'd been The Organization's slave. It was imperative the persona he'd built since his escape ten years ago remained unimpeachable. He wasn't letting anything threaten his chances of reclaiming his heritage.

To that end, he had to follow this society's rules until they became second nature to him. As they were to Megumi and her family. The family that had no idea *he* was one of them.

They'd never find out he was. But he would become one of them. He'd become a Hashimoto through marriage to—

Suddenly, a jolt speared through his body. It originated at his nape and forked down to his toes.

But the all-out alarm wasn't one of danger. He was versed in recognizing threats. This red alert was one of awareness.

Without any change in expression or posture,

he threw the net of his senses out before yanking it back, eliminating everything but the source of the disturbance.

The next second, Megumi gripped his forearm.

He frowned. Megumi never touched him. So had his reaction been in anticipation of her touch? But why would she suddenly wring such a jarring response from him?

Turning his gaze down to her, he was relieved to feel no reaction to her sight and now touch, as usual. But the awareness searing through him was intensifying. It took all his control not to look around for its origin.

"Matsuyama-san is approaching."

So that was why she'd grabbed him so urgently—to draw his attention to the approach of their host. Hiro Matsuyama. The man who'd gone all-out holding this ball in his mansion. And his bitterest business rival in Japan.

It still felt weird being honored by an adversary. But that was an expected ritual in Japan. A necessary one even. Tradition and decorum were valued above all in business as in society. It would take him a while to get used to that, along with everything else, as he hadn't been raised Japanese.

But then, he hadn't been raised at all. From the age of four years old, he'd been forged. Into a lethal weapon.

He let adversaries glimpse that side of him to keep them in check, showing them what they were really up against. But though Hiro posed his biggest business threat, compared with the monsters Raiden had vanquished in his time, Hiro was harmless. No, his senses couldn't be going haywire to herald his approach.

Turning to Megumi, he saw her eyes fixed, vaguely noted the glazed look in them, the tremor in her lower lip. His focus left her behind as the disruption grew in intensity.

Then he was facing Hiro…and the woman he had on his arm. And the realization was instantaneous.

She was the source of the disturbance.

She was the only female around who wasn't Japanese. Even the non-Japanese businessmen in attendance were married to Japanese women. It was the only way to truly enter society, the path to the most solid form of business alliances in Japan.

Every eye in the ballroom seemed to be following her. The Japanese had strict parameters for their women's beauty. But most were enamored with Caucasian beauty and coloring. Most men obsessed about Western women, even if few approached them, because many of the qualities they so admired in the safety of fantasy proved intimidating in reality. All of those qualities were present in this woman.

She towered above everyone, flaunted her height even more with high heels. Hiro was tall for a Japanese man at almost six feet, and she stood taller. Only a couple of inches short of looking six-foot-four Raiden in the eyes.

She stood out in every other way, too. Among all the dark-haired people around, she looked like a flame-haired Amazon, tanned, curvaceous, bodacious, oozing sexuality and confidence. And among all the women in soft or bright colors, she was the only one in fathomless black. She looked every voluptuous inch the femme fatale, the opposite of everything considered desirable in a Japanese woman, the antithesis of the petite, porcelain-skinned, delicate and demure Megumi. Though one look at prevalent Japanese porn said she was the epitome of the nation's not-so-secret fantasies.

But he didn't share those fantasies, had none really. That came from the total discipline he'd trained in from early childhood, to hone his skills to inhuman precision. During his years with The Organization, he hadn't made use of the choice female companionship they'd provided to keep their agents placated. Since his escape, he'd remained as fastidious. The one time his shields had come crashing down had been with *her.*

But *this* woman was evoking the same…compulsion. When she wasn't even looking at him.

His awareness clung to her even as he forced his gaze to pan to Hiro as he bowed to Megumi. Raiden barely registered that her hand dug deeper into his forearm. Everything in him was focused on the other woman.

Hiro bowed stiltedly in answer to his own compulsory bow, before resuming looking at Megumi. "May I introduce Ms. Scarlett Delacroix, Megumi-san?"

As the ladies exchanged bows, his eyes were dragged back to the woman's profile. He barely tore them away as Hiro turned to him, his gaze colliding with his, the arm around Scarlett Delacroix's nipped waist visibly tightening.

Was Hiro announcing his claim? Telling Raiden not to think of making a move? Hiro assumed he would, with his brand-new fiancée standing at his side?

That would make Hiro more astute than Raiden had thought. He did want to make a move. Which stunned him, because he never did.

But maybe Hiro wasn't reading his aberrant reaction specifically, just believed Scarlett Delacroix was irresistible to any male. He would be right about that, too. If he with his ironclad control felt those unstoppable urges toward that vivid creature, other men must be champing at the bit.

But his reaction was indeed abnormal. He waded in gorgeous women and gave none a second glance. But this woman's effect had nothing to do with her physical attributes. It was identical to *her* effect. His every sense was clamoring so loud, as if in recognition...

This was beyond pathetic. Projecting his reactions to a long-gone and deceitful lover onto other women.

But then he'd never had anything approaching this reaction to any other woman. It was only this woman, this Scarlett....

"Scarlett, please meet Raiden Kuroshiro."

Hiro's grudging introduction yanked him out of his insane musings to find her extending her hand. His rose involuntarily to meet it...and static sparked at their touch.

Her hand lurched away, a gasp escaping her full lips, before they spread in an exquisite bow. "Serves me right for going for an all-synthetic, antiwrinkle gown," she said, explaining away the spark. "Now I need grounding."

Her accent was American, her voice too low to fathom clearly in the background din, but its warmth speared through his loins, made him grit his teeth.

Hiro pulled her more securely to his side. "It must be a mere manifestation of your electrifying personality."

Raiden aborted a snort at Hiro's hackneyed comment. But what he couldn't rein in was his rising hackles at Hiro's possessive attitude. He couldn't believe his reaction. He'd *never* felt confrontational with another man over a woman.

Then she turned fully to him, the smile on her lips not reaching her eyes as they met his for the first time. The bolt that hit him this time almost rocked him on his feet.

Those eyes. Those intense, luminescent sapphire blues. They were the same color of *her* eyes.

It was really getting ridiculous how he was trying to find similarities between the two completely different women.

"I hear congratulations are in order," Scarlett murmured, her gaze flitting from his eyes to Megumi's before he could hold it.

It couldn't be she was shy. This was a woman who knew her power over men, a power that must have been perfected through years of practice and exercised at will. He was certain there wasn't a diffident cell in that voluptuous body. So why didn't she want to look him in the eye?

"Scarlett had a prior engagement." Hiro turned

to Scarlett, his gaze taking on a besotted edge. "But she still honored me with consenting to grace the ball."

"How could I not, when you organize the best balls in the northern hemisphere, Hiro?" Scarlett turned to Megumi with a warm smile. "Between you and me, I was hoping that by meeting the guests of honor of this ball, I might get my first invitation to a high-society Japanese wedding."

"If I'm invited—" Hiro shot Megumi a brief glance before resuming his adoration of Scarlett "—you certainly will be."

"We'd be honored to have you both grace the wedding." Megumi felt nowhere her usual serene self, her words brittle, her expression forced.

She didn't like Scarlett? Probably not many women did. Scarlett must be an ego crusher, especially to those females who considered themselves beautiful. For she was magnificent.

"I trust this is also Kuroshiro-san's sentiment?" Hiro asked, turning his challenging gaze to him.

In their previous meetings, Hiro had been reserved, but he'd made it clear their enmity would be kept to the financial battlefield. This time, though, he was struggling to hold back his aggression. Because he felt territorial over Scarlett?

Not that she'd given Hiro any reason to fear him. She'd barely looked in his direction so far.

Hiro, on the other hand, was still glaring at him, waiting for his corroboration. Raiden gave it to him with an inclination of his head.

Megumi's hand tightened. Was she urging him to vocalize his response? He knew he had to comply, or it would be taken as an offense. His silence so far had been bad enough.

He didn't feel like making a response. Right now the only thing he felt like doing was snatching Hiro's arm off Scarlett's waist and dragging her away from him.

Still, he said, "Matsuyama-san, Ms. Delacroix, your presence at our wedding isn't only our privilege, it's a necessity."

His deferential words didn't seem to appease Hiro. The man's response was perplexing, since Hiro had not only insisted on holding this ball, but had brought to his attention the very woman he was visually wrestling him over.

Thankfully, the stilted meeting came to an end

shortly afterward, and Hiro and Scarlett moved on. Raiden forced himself not to watch them walk away. Not to watch *her*. But he could no longer bear having Megumi by his side.

Looking down at her, he tried to smile, failing this time. "If it's okay with you, Megumi, I'll now take advantage of your kind offer to go make the rounds."

"Of course." Megumi stepped back, looking as relieved as he felt to finally separate.

Walking away, he forced himself to stop by a few congratulators. As soon as he saw an opening to get out of the ballroom, he took it. On his way out, he again saw Scarlett. She was heading out, too. Even from the back, and from a distance, the sense of familiarity swamped him all over again. The same intensity he'd experienced when he'd first seen *her*.

Her. That was how he'd always thought of the woman he'd known by the name of Hannah McPherson.

He'd met her in New York one bright summer afternoon five years ago, when she'd swerved her car to avoid hitting a reckless biker and crashed into his car instead.

From the moment she'd stepped out of her car, everything else had ceased to matter to him. The inexorable attraction he'd felt toward her had been something he'd never thought he could experience. He'd always told her she'd literally crashed into his life, and pulverized all his pre-conceptions and rules.

Ignoring his usual precautions, he hadn't even performed the most basic investigation on her. It had been through her that he'd known her to be a kindergarten teacher by morning, and a florist who ran an inherited shop by afternoon.

When he'd taken her out that first night, she'd made it clear it wouldn't go any further because he inhabited a world alien to hers. She hadn't budged when he'd insisted that attraction like theirs bridged all differences. It had taken their first kiss for her to capitulate, concede that what had sprung between them had been unstoppable. And from that first night, he'd plunged with her into an incendiary affair.

Then after five delirious months, a single in-explicable discrepancy had led him to unravel an ingeniously spun web of fraud. And to an appalling verdict. That her identity had been manufactured just prior to meeting him.

It had all been a setup. Starting with the accident that had brought them together. She must have been sent by some rival to spy on him. And in their intimacy, he'd left himself wide-open. Whatever she'd been after, she could have found it.

But since no one had used privileged information against him yet, either she hadn't found what she'd been looking for or she was waiting for the right time to leverage her intel from her recruiters. Or him. Or both.

Pretending to be oblivious until he'd decided how to deal with her, he'd called her. She'd been her usual bright, eager self at first, then as if hearing through his act, her voice had changed, becoming a stranger's. Then she'd asked if he preferred she called him Lightning, or if he'd left that name behind when he'd escaped The Organization. And he'd realized it had been far worse than his worst fears.

It hadn't been corporate espionage material she'd managed to get her hands on, but his most lethal secret. His previous identity. And she'd known its value, its danger. That its exposure would bring The Organization to his and his brothers' doors. The Organization that needed them all dead.

His blood had frozen and boiled at once as she'd said it was just as well he'd brought the charade to an end so she could make her demands. Some money in exchange for her silence.

"Some money" had turned out to be fifty million dollars.

Enraged, he'd assured her he didn't negotiate with blackmailers. He took them out. So it was in *her* best interest to keep what she knew to herself.

Unfazed by his threat, she'd said he'd never find her to carry it out, but that she'd had no wish to expose him, just needed the money. It was pocket change to him, so he should just pay without involving payback or pride. He also shouldn't fear she'd ever ask for more or hold her knowledge over him in any other way. Once the transaction was complete, he could consider that she'd never existed. As she'd never truly had.

Though bitterness and fury had consumed him, cold logic had said that while he couldn't trust his instincts or her, he could trust her sense of self-preservation. She'd already known how lethal he could be, and she wouldn't risk extorting him again. This would be a one-off thing. It would end this catastrophic breach to his and his brothers' security.

But he'd found himself wondering. If she really needed the money, he'd gladly help her, if only she'd tell him she'd been forced to spy on him, and that it hadn't been all a lie.

His need to look the other way in return for such a reassurance had made him even angrier. At himself. Deciding to end the sordid interlude, he'd transferred the money to the offshore account she'd provided, what had been untraceable even to his formidable resources. As per her declaration, he'd never found any trace of her again. It *had* been as if she'd never existed. It had been truly over.

But it hadn't ended. Not for him.

His obsession with her continued to torment him. It sank its talons the deepest when he was at his lowest ebb. It was at such times he yearned to turn to her, the only woman who'd touched his innermost being, to feel her vitality filling his arms, her empathy touching his soul, her passion igniting his cravings. Every time, he'd cursed her even more, for needing her still.

But his anger remained mostly directed at himself—the master of stealth who'd failed to detect the least trace of duplicity in her. And who, even after it had been proved, had remained inextricably under her spell.

Shaking himself out of the bitter musings, he now exited the ballroom in pursuit of that other woman who had wrung the same reactions from him.

Scarlett Delacroix was gracefully gliding across the mansion's expansive terrace, descending the stairs to the traditional tea garden. In the light of a gibbous moon, her red tresses were the only splash of color and heat in the scene's monotone coldness. The layered skirt of her black dress trailed after her like a piece of night that worshipped her lush figure.

Noting that Hiro's bodyguards were monitoring her progress, he waited as she crossed the wooden bridge to the garden house, then set off in the opposite direction.

In minutes, he entered the building soundlessly

from its southern entrance. The warmth of the interior advanced as if to greet him, but it was her aura that reached out and enveloped him as she stood looking out the screen window.

It was uncanny. His reaction to her was identical to his reaction to Hannah, when physically she couldn't be more different. Still, he couldn't shake that insane feeling. Or resist the preposterous impulse.

He stepped out of the shadows and strode toward her.

Without turning, she only shot him a sidelong glance. There was no doubt about it. She'd felt him there all along, had been waiting for him to make a move.

His heat rose as she resumed looking out to the exquisite moonlit garden. No one, no woman, certainly not Hannah, had ever treated him with such nonchalance.

He stopped a breath away, bent and placed his lips an inch from her ear. His words rustled the hair tucked behind it. "Why are you out here and not in that ballroom soaking up the collective adulation?"

Without giving any indication if his nearness

affected her in any way, she said, "Not that I noticed such generalized fascination, but I came out for some fresh air and solitude. I'm a touch claustrophobic *and* agoraphobic. A full ballroom is my ultimate aversion."

"Is it? Or are you just giving Hiro something he's never experienced—a woman who can leave his side, who isn't trying to court his favor with her every breath? If you walked away to test how deep your hook has sunk into him, are you now disappointed he hasn't come running after you?"

"I plead not guilty to all of your assumptions, Mr. Kuroshiro. But the question is, why are *you* here? Why aren't you back in that ballroom collecting oaths of allegiance and obedience? Can I assume my so-called hook has inadvertently sunk in you instead, and it has brought *you* running after me?"

"You can indeed assume, Ms. Delacroix." He paused for a second, then decided to act on the unstoppable compulsion, no matter how absurd it was. "Or should I say Ms. McPherson?"

For an interminable stretch, there was absolutely no reaction from her. Nothing but total stillness and silence.

Then she turned her head to him, her heavily fringed, vibrantly blue eyes looking up at him in what looked like amusement. "I heard that right, didn't I? You just implied I'm someone else? Someone you know?" A brief, tinkling chuckle escaped her dimpled lips. "That's one line I was never given."

His hands itched to clamp over the flesh that pulled at his instincts like inexorable gravity. He barely fought the temptation. "Because men approach you with protests that you're like no one they'd ever met? Take heart. You're still unique. So much so, even a totally different face and body didn't stop me from recognizing you."

There. The words were out. And they sounded ludicrous. At least, to his logic. His instincts said different. He'd follow those wherever they willed until it all played out.

Her eyebrows rose in incredulity before a considering expression came into her eyes. "Is this a game? You want me to pretend I'm this… McPherson woman? And will you be someone else, too? Someone free to indulge himself with a total stranger?" She turned fully to him, leaned back against the window frame over arms tucked behind her back. "I did hear role-playing is huge in Japan, but I wouldn't have thought you're the type who'd be into it. But then, maybe you're just that. Someone who became a billionaire so young must lead a very stressful life. Maybe it's your preferred method of defusing the pressures."

Her every calm syllable, her steady gaze, made everything inside him churn.

His lips twisted grimly, mocking his runaway reaction, conceding her effect. "Your on-the-fly performance is impressive. But then, you always *were* the most spontaneous, undetectable imposter I've ever encountered."

Only one delicately curved auburn eyebrow rose this time, and what seemed so much like real interest entered her gaze. "Have you encountered that many?"

"Hundreds. And I've seen through each of them at a hundred paces. It was only you who took me in, all the way. But I'm now immunized for life against falling for your charades again."

She shook her head as if she'd had enough of playing his game. Then suddenly she tilted it at him, her gaze shedding its mockery, becoming smoldering. "You don't need an outrageous approach to hook me, Mr. Kuroshiro. I'm already interested."

That was something he hadn't expected her to say. Not that he'd expected anything. He was flying blind here.

"You are?"

"Every female with only a brain wave would be." She sighed. "Pity you're engaged."

"Does that even matter?"

"I guess it wouldn't to someone like you. Even if I suspect that such a someone doesn't exist, that you're one of a kind. I expect you're bound by no rules and consider no one in your decisions."

"You already know this about me."

"You mean this McPherson woman knows this about you."

"Will you keep pretending you're not her for long?"

She sighed again. "I already told you I'm interested. And since being engaged doesn't deter you, it's something actually in your favor, since you must only want something intense…and transient. The only kind of liaison I'm open to."

"So Hiro hasn't reserved a place in your bed yet?"

"Hiro, like everything else in my life, is of no concern to you and is off-limits to discussion. I do as I please, and no one has any claims on me."

"I bet Hiro doesn't know this part. Or he does, and you're still dangling the bait. And while you wait until he swallows the whole fishing rod, you welcome diversions?"

"Why not? I'm a free agent so far." She uncoiled to her full statuesque height. "But I've had enough of indulging your role-playing fetish. Let's revisit this when you decide to talk to me, not your imaginary character."

Without lingering one more second, she turned away. He watched her receding, a flame-haired goddess of the night dissolving into her domain, his thoughts tangling.

Had he made a gigantic fool of himself? All evidence said so. His instincts, however, still screamed their contradictory verdict.

Exasperation rumbled from his gut as he lunged after her, grabbed her by the waist and slammed her against his length.

A gasp swelled in her chest as he stabbed a

hand into the heavy silk at her nape, tethering her head. In the golden illumination of fire-lit lanterns, her eyes held his in utmost composure, belying her ragged moan at his roughness. And he crashed his lips over hers, swallowing the intoxicating sound.

Her lips parted wide under his onslaught, letting him plunge into her depths, her flesh softening to accommodate his impacting hardness. Her surrender blazed through his nerves. But it was certainty that singed his every cell.

This. This was *her* unforgotten feel and taste, *her* inimitable delight. This *was* her.

The beast that had been perpetually clawing inside him finally tore free. It devoured her, everything inside him roaring with remembrance. Of every minute of deprivation of the five years after she'd left him. Craving more. Needing closure.

Then it swelled. Disgust. With himself. Over the only weakness he'd ever suffered, this susceptibility to her. It towered, then crashed, made him tear his lips from hers, push away from the body that had seemed to melt into his every recess.

Stumbling back at the abruptness of his withdrawal, she leaned against the nearest wall, the only discernible reaction to his explosive kiss her faster breathing.

Then, through those lips he'd just ravished, her voice washed over him, calm, collected… but *hers* at last.

"What gave me away?"

Two

"Everything."

The word boomed in the silence of the garden house. Its reverberations hung in the charged air between them, dripping with bitterness, heavy with five years of unresolved anger.

Not even a blip in her gaze or posture demonstrated any agitation. Only a slight tremor of her now-swollen lips betrayed any reaction to his fury. One that stilled at once, making him think he'd imagined it.

Which he probably had. Meeting him hadn't fazed her at all. And why should it have? She'd come to the ball knowing she'd see him. It was he who'd gotten the shock of his life.

Then, as calmly, she said, "We both know that can't be true. Not even I recognize the woman who looks back at me in the mirror as myself."

She was right. Even on such close-up inspection, there wasn't the least trace of his treacherous lover in her. He'd changed his looks to eliminate perfect resemblance to his old self, but she had totally different facial features and bone structure. Even her complexion looked different. Hannah had had alabaster skin, the kind he'd thought would burn, not tan. But this Scarlett's tan looked effortless, her skin even, velvet honey. And the deep shade of burgundy of her hair looked natural, too, when Hannah had been an equally convincing platinum blonde. All those changes were certainly artificial, even if their result looked 100 percent real. The only changes that could be natural were her body's. Maturity and heels could account for the appreciation in her curves and height.

But all in all, this woman bore no resemblance to the one who'd been in his bed every day of those five months, whose every inch he'd memorized and worshipped.

He cocked his head at her, drenching her from

head to toe in disdain. "I assume this is my money's worth? This total and undetectable transformation?"

Her expression remained tranquil, assessing him back. "I wouldn't call it undetectable. At least, not anymore. You detected me." She let out a conceding sigh. "I did have some incredibly costly surgeries to reconfigure my face from the bone structure up. And though your money did foot the bills, along with the other cosmetic and stylistic measures needed to complete the transformation, not even all that cost anywhere near fifty million dollars. The whole thing cost around two million. A couple more financed the creation of my new identity with a whole history and paper trail for it."

"So you still have millions to spare. Or did you invest those into billions? Was that how you got into Hiro's inner circle, through the doors only that kind of money opens?"

Her lashes lowered before rising to strike him with a flash of azure. "I sort of…crashed my way into that."

His simmering blood tumbled in a boil.

"So you're still using your old tried-and-true methods."

"Why change what works?" Suddenly her expression became distant, as if reversing into the past to the crash she'd manufactured to enter *his* life. "It was a different sort of crash." Her eyes refocused on him, resumed being supremely placid. "Even if just as effective. But though I put your money to the best use possible, alas, the Midas touch that turns millions into ever-increasing billions remains firmly yours."

Teeth gritting, he bunched hands stinging with the need to grab her again at his sides. "You seem very much at ease with divulging your machinations and secrets now."

A graceful shoulder rose in an easy shrug. "You already found me out. And I'm still waiting to hear how you did."

"It was your eyes."

Those eyes filled with mock reprimand. "They were what I worked on most, so I'm pretty sure they're unrecognizable."

"I recognized the color."

"You can't possibly have recognized me from just that."

"It's a unique color, and changes hue in as unique a way. I used to be fascinated by its fluctuations, thought they corresponded to shifts in your emotions. Then I found out you have none, and those were just a response to variations in lighting."

A still moment, then a tinge of sarcasm entered those eyes that *were* totally different, yet, to him, somehow exactly the same. "Are you telling me I owe being exposed to a fixation you had with my eye color and some trick of light I wasn't even aware of? And you're sticking with that story?"

"I *felt* you."

His hiss wiped the provocation off her face. She'd cornered him into admitting her relentless hold over him, and that even without evidence, he'd always know her.

Now that the admission was out, he might as well go all the way. "I felt you before I turned to see you on Hiro's arm. Not even millions of dollars' worth of permanent disguise was able to wipe off the inimitable imprint you left on my senses." He cocked his head, his gaze spearing hers. "How about that story? You find it more plausible? More satisfactory?"

Her gaze had emptied, and now her voice followed suit. "I had no idea I'd left such an indelible mark. It's why I thought it okay to come here tonight. I thought there was no danger you'd sense the least familiarity, let alone recognize me outright. I met many people who knew me well in my previous…incarnations, and none even felt any vague resemblance."

"I'm not 'people.'"

Her nod conceded that. "I know in *your* previous incarnation you were said to have senses so acute, it made you a ninja in a class of your own. I couldn't tell if those reports were exaggerations. Now I know they weren't."

"You had reason to believe they were outright lies, with the way said senses were disabled around you. I had no inkling of your deceit for five straight months of ultimate intimacy."

Her fixed glance remained unchanged as her head tilted to one side, sending the curtain of her loose silk curls swishing over her polished shoulder. "Speaking of that, I always wondered what finally gave me away *that* time."

He was damned if he'd give her the satisfaction, and the security, of knowing it had been total chance that had finally alerted him, and not his allegedly infallible abilities.

"You want to find out so you'll never repeat the lapse, hone your deception powers to perfection? Sorry, you'll have to keep on wondering. And worrying."

"Oh, I never worry. Even in the rare times I slip up, I always manage to compensate. As I did when I preempted you."

How she'd realized he'd found her out back then had remained a major question mark. Needing an answer to it had even outstripped his need to find his lineage in the past years.

Wrestling with the urge to pounce on her and force her to tell him now, he tried to match her nonchalance. "And now? How will you preempt me this time?"

A sigh accompanied a regretful shake of that elegant head. "It really would have been better for everyone if you didn't recognize me."

"Everyone meaning you."

"Everyone meaning everyone. Starting by you."

A vicious huff crackled from his depths.

"You're implying knowing your real identity poses danger to me, too?"

"It poses danger to you…only." Before he processed that outrageous statement, she added, "And you don't know my real identity."

Giving in, he obliterated the distance he'd put between them. He needed a physical reinforcement of his dominance, feeling he was on the losing side of this confrontation.

He regretted it the moment he drew his next breath. Though she'd been so thorough in her disguise to the point of changing the soap and perfume she'd used before, her own scent deluged him, even through the masking of new adornments. Hot, vital, intoxicating. The exact bouquet that had been the only one to activate his libido.

Glaring down at her, as if it would shift the balance of power in his favor, he said, "I know this one is fabricated. As was the one before it. Which should be enough. So explain to me how this knowledge, when it's clearly a secret you've kept from everyone here, wouldn't impact you."

"It *would* cause me intense inconvenience. But it's you who stands to suffer major damage if you expose me." Before he scoffed at that preposterous declaration, she asked, "But really, why would you want to expose me at all?"

"To stop you from setting Hiro up."

After a moment, when it looked as if she didn't get his meaning, incredulity coated her face. "What makes you think I'm doing any such thing? Because you consider I set *you* up?"

"And you don't? What do you call what you did to me?" He waved, stopping any argument in its tracks. Haggling over facts turned them into points of view that could be contested and rewritten. And he was damned if he'd let her do that. "Whatever you're doing, it's criminal."

"Because I'm withholding my real identity? Pot calling the kettle black much?" Her full lips twisted. "And if you're citing my past actions in your unsubstantiated accusations, I did nothing criminal with you. I actually…helped you."

It was his turn to cough in disbelief. "Sure, by systematically deceiving me for five months, then leaving a fifty-million-dollar gaping hole in my liquid assets. I bet that's every man's idea of 'help.'"

"It isn't a crime to con a con man. I was sent

to expose an assassin who was posing as a squeaky-clean businessman. The only crimes were in *your* past, not mine."

He gaped at her, astounded all over again. Even after he'd found out she'd conned him, after she'd blackmailed him, he'd thought she'd held her own with him only because he'd been in a precarious position, and more important, because they'd had their confrontation over the phone. If they'd been face-to-face, he'd always thought she wouldn't have been able to maintain her poise.

But this woman with the steely self-possession could stare down the scariest monsters he'd ever dealt with and not turn a hair. If she could hold him at a disadvantage with such effortlessness when he'd thought she would be vulnerable and off balance, no one else would stand a chance against her.

He shook his head. "I didn't choose my old persona. It wasn't the real me. This new one I created is. I bet you can't say the same about yourself. So whatever you call what you do for a living, I call you a professional fraud, out of choice. And whatever elaborate deception you're perpetrating now, I will stop you. I let you get away with deceiving me once. I'm not letting you get away with anything again."

He'd let his lethal side surface as he talked. Expecting exposure to it to shake her at last, he was again amazed when she met his menace head-on.

"You can only 'stop' me if you expose me. And you can't, because it would mean exposing yourself."

He coughed in incredulity. "Are you threatening me?"

"*You're* the one who's threatening to strike me down like your old code name. I'm just pointing out that your righteousness is blinding you to the fact that it's in your best interests to keep my secrets. Why do you think I was so free with them?"

"Because you think I can't do anything with what I know?"

"Not if you want what *I* know to remain buried."

"You *are* threatening me, then."

Something like exasperation tinged her gaze. "I once promised I'd never hold my knowledge over you, and I remain at my word." When he glowered at her, failing to find any words to express what collided inside his head and chest, she exhaled. "Listen, Raiden, you're the one who can create this impasse, and you mustn't. Not when you're mere steps from attaining the family and the status you've craved all your life."

His heart convulsed. She knew this?

Though it shocked him, it stood to reason. Through his obliviousness, his misplaced trust, this woman had somehow once found out his every secret. It must have been easy for someone of her shrewdness to extrapolate his life goals and future plans. Now that she knew the arrangement he had with Megumi and her father, as it had been announced in society already, the details must have been as obvious to her.

It made sense, but it still galled him that she knew so much about him when he knew nothing about her, except what she made him feel, how she still had such power over him.

As if reading his mind, something like gentle persuasion entered her gaze. "Whatever you feel about me, no matter your burning desire to punish me for my transgressions against you, I'm not worth tarnishing the perfect image you've worked so hard and long to create. And that would certainly happen if you expose me. For what would you say I blackmailed you for? You can't say that you succumbed to my blackmail, since it would make you look weak, or that you needed to hide something that badly. If you expose me anonymously, once the mess is out in the open, details have a way of surfacing, of becoming land mines you never know which step will set off."

Fury, and something else he hadn't felt since he was a child—futility—mushroomed inside him.

Everything she'd said was true. Any action against her now, in this delicate time, would have consequences, and the fallout would inescapably harm him. If not now, then later. Whatever impacted him, it would surely drag his brothers in by association. So he couldn't act on the burning desire to punish her, as she'd so accurately put it.

When he made no response, she prodded, that same chafing gentleness in her tone. "Why don't you let me be and go about your business? Your wedding and adopting your family name are just over two months from now, and you can't afford to let anything sabotage that."

She was right again. Damn her.

But there was one thing he wasn't backing down from. "I will let you be, on one condition. That you keep away from Hiro. I'm not letting you exploit him as you did me."

It seemed he had finally managed to surprise her. Her eyes, those eyes that in spite of everything he wanted to drown in, widened. "You're really worried about him? I thought, as his number one rival, you'd welcome whatever misfortune befell him."

"I certainly wouldn't. I fight my adversaries with merit. I wouldn't want to win dishonorably."

"It wouldn't be dishonorable if someone else felled him for you."

"It would be if I knew of his jeopardy and looked the other way. And I won't."

"This *is* about honor, isn't it? You're really taking integrating into your new society to the limit, huh?"

"You may never understand what honor is, but it's the most important thing to me, and I would do anything to satisfy mine. Even if it means risking my plans."

He held her incandescent gaze as it fluctuated through the range of blue-and-violet spectrum in the softly shifting lights. He imbued his own with his contempt, and his conviction.

She finally shook her head. "You don't have to do that. And you don't have to worry about Hiro. I'd never hurt him."

A skewer twisted in his gut. The way she'd said that… That look in her eyes… It was as if she truly cared for Hiro.

Then the icicles of memory sank into his core, numbing the ache. She'd once looked at him with the same profound emotions. Her ability to project genuineness was unheard of. She could be doing the same now. She must be.

"I can almost see you rejecting what I just said as more fraud." Her eyes were opaque, her voice hushed. "I can't do anything about that, but I can about something else. Before anyone realizes you're here with me, leaving your fiancée back there, and you cause yourself unneeded scandal, I'll do you a favor and do what you seem unable to do. I'll walk away. Let me do that and you can forget all about me again."

With that, she strode to the door she'd entered from. At the threshold, she paused, turned, and the crisp night wind blew her hair toward him like tongues of flame.

Before he could storm after her as every cell in his body was screaming for him to, her voice carried to him across the still warmth, lilting, husky, exactly what had poured into his brain on their transfiguring nights of passion.

"You won't believe this either, Raiden, but it was…nice seeing you again. This time, I at least get to say goodbye."

Scarlett walked away steadily. Her five-inch heels clicked on the wooden bridge leading away from the garden house over the pond in a rhythmic, deliberate staccato.

Inside her, absolute chaos raged.

This confrontation with Raiden had been a total shock. It hadn't even been a possibility in her mind coming here.

When Hiro had called her a few hours ago, insisting that she attended this ball, she'd been loath to agree. Even with a new face and identity, she dreaded social functions and suffocated under scrutiny. Looking the way she did now, and being a gaijin, as foreigners were called in Japan, and Hiro's personal companion to boot, she'd been certain she'd be put under the microscope of public interest. But she'd agreed without letting Hiro know of her aversion. She'd do anything for him.

Then he'd told her he was sending her the dress he wanted her to wear, and her dormant curiosity had been roused. But it had been when she'd noticed he'd sounded nothing like his warmly indulgent and coolly humorous self, but nervous, urgent and sour, that she'd gently probed.

And he'd told her what he'd withheld from her for months—why he'd been holding this ball, and for whom. The woman he wanted. She'd become engaged to another, obeying her family's demands. He'd wanted to show her he wouldn't be mourning her loss, had an exotic beauty on whom to bestow the affections she'd rejected. Then he'd told her the name of the man he'd lost his woman to. Raiden.

After that, she'd been as anxious as he about this ball.

During the past three years, after she'd resurfaced with her new identity, she'd seen Raiden many times, all from afar. He'd even been the indirect reason she'd come to Japan. Seeing him up close again was a whole different ball game, the anticipation eating her up with agitation and eagerness.

So she'd dressed up as Hiro had wanted, played the role he'd wanted her to play when he'd taken her to Raiden and his fiancée. Empathy at Hiro's suffering at Megumi's sight had been intensified by her upheaval at Raiden's nearness. Seeing him face-to-face had felt like a direct blow to the heart.

But she'd played her part for Hiro's sake, and had almost sagged in his stiff hold when he, too, hadn't been able to bear Megumi's nearness any longer and cut their confrontation short. She'd thought that had been it.

Not for a second had she considered Raiden might see any similarity between the new her and the casually dressing, flat shoe–wearing, slim blonde he'd once known. So even when she'd felt him following her, she'd thought he'd been pursuing Hiro's new romantic interest. The Raiden she'd known wouldn't have struck at an adversary that way, but then he could have changed since she'd betrayed him.

Then he'd confronted her, and every meticulously erected pillar maintaining her cohesion had crumbled in shock.

But she'd been trained too well, through too many brutal tests. She'd acted her way to perfection through her life's worst situations. And she'd had plenty of nightmarish ones. None, however, had ever affected her as her time with Raiden had.

In the garden house, she'd still fallen back on her fail-safe maneuvers, trapping her agitation in her deepest recesses, plastering one of her automated reaction modes on the surface. But then he'd taken her in his arms, drowned her in a kiss that had dissolved the last vestiges of her facade. And she'd given up the pretense.

What had followed had been agonizing. But she hoped she'd maintained a semblance of indifference all through.

One thing held her together now as she walked

away from Raiden. Knowing that he'd heed her warning and leave her alone. She'd never see or hear from him again. Or if she did, he'd pretend she was the total stranger he'd just met tonight.

Not that he didn't hate it. She'd felt him seething to obey the urge to do her major damage, equivalent to what he considered she'd caused him. She could feel his gaze on her all the way to the mansion's entrance, bombarding her with his pent-up rage and contempt.

By the time she reached one of Hiro's limos, she'd expended the last of her balance. After forcing her rented apartment's address in Shibuya out of unsteady lips to the unknown driver, she flopped back in her seat, her nerves in pieces, her muscles like trembling jelly.

Exhaling forcibly to expel her agitation, she tried to luxuriate in the sights of Tokyo at night. The city was one of the most exotic and exciting places she'd ever been, and her life had taken her almost everywhere.

She soon gave up, resigned she'd see nothing during the hour's drive but Raiden's magnificent, wrathful face. Would feel nothing but regurgitated turmoil and searing memories.

Had it really been five years? The insane whirl-pool of events as she'd reinvented herself since made her feel as if it had been fifty years. But his memory was so intense, it could have been five days since she'd last seen him. She hadn't forgotten a thing about him. His beauty was as indescribable as she remembered, and his effect on her was as overpowering.

When she'd been sent to spy on him, all she'd known was that he was an American billion-aire venture capitalist of Japanese origins. His business past was impeccable and his personal one unremarkable, having been born to a single mother who'd died when he'd been ten, placing him in the foster system until he'd been eighteen. Then he'd traveled the world before coming back to the States at twenty-six, and he'd been soar-ing through the venture capitalism field since. He'd been twenty-nine when she'd met him and already a billionaire. Now at thirty-four, he was at the undisputable top, with a handful of oth-ers, one of whom was Hiro.

But her recruiter was convinced Raiden was a former assassin, and had sent her to get intimate with Raiden and get solid proof. And she had.

Through the full access Raiden had given her to his domain, she'd used her special training to breach his secret records and gotten that proof.

But it had been years of research later that had put together his real life story. What he himself hadn't known when he'd been with her. It had been just months ago that she'd worked out just how he'd become that ninja assassin called Lightning.

He'd been two when he'd lost his family in an earthquake and tsunami that hit the rural Akita Prefecture in Japan. Taken to a shelter in the aftermath, he'd remained there for two years until his extraordinary agility had brought him to the attention of a "recruiter" for The Organization, a shadow operation that took children and turned them into unstoppable mercenaries who executed top-risk operations for the highest bidders. Pretending she was a relative, the recruiter had taken him only to sell him to The Organization.

He'd been among hundreds of boys taken from all over the world, kept segregated in a remote area in the Balkans, viciously trained and molded until they graduated to fieldwork. They performed missions under strict surveillance from their personal handlers. Death was the only punishment for any attempts at subordination or escape. But he'd been one of a few who'd ever escaped. She suspected some or even all of his partners in Black Castle Enterprises were also escapees.

She'd often wondered if he'd called himself Raiden, the god of thunder and lightning in Japan, to reflect his code name when he'd been the ultimate ninja warrior, so certain no one would ever tie him to his former identity. His cover *was* ingenious, after all, and it *was* a common enough name. As for Kuroshiro, that literally meant Black Castle. She'd also wondered if he'd picked it after the name of his joint enterprise with his partners, or if they'd taken his....

Suddenly she almost spilled out of the limo. Her driver had opened her door. She hadn't even noticed they'd stopped.

Pulling herself together and out of the past, she thanked him, stepped out and walked into her building.

Looking around the chic foyer on her way to the elevator and her thirtieth-floor unit, she felt thankful all over again to Hiro for making it possible for her to be here.

When she'd first come to Japan just over a year ago and tried to rent a place, she'd learned what the Japanese phrase *hikoshi bimbo* meant. It literally meant "moving poor." The humongous sum of cash that renters had to dish out up front invariably left them impoverished.

Since she'd had no cash in any sums, it hadn't been an option. After she'd met Hiro, and he'd discovered she'd been sleeping on the floor of the UNICEF regional office where she worked, he'd been appalled and insisted on accommodating her.

She'd refused to stay in his mansion, since being in someone's debt and in their domain was anathema to her. Autonomy and seclusion were a vital necessity to her. She'd also declined the exorbitant apartment he'd gotten her near his home. He'd protested that he had billions, was still around to spend them only thanks to her. She'd argued that even if the place came for free, it was too far from her work downtown.

In the end, he'd still gotten her a "mansion," as recently built large apartments were called in

Tokyo. The place was expensive, but now that she did some part-time consulting work for him, she could accept the home in lieu of a salary.

She now entered the apartment, sighed in pleasure at feeling cocooned in its sound-insulated exquisite mixture of modern and traditional Japanese ambiance. Kicking off her towering sandals, she moaned in relief as her feet flattened against the *tatami,* the traditional Japanese flooring made of rice straw with a covering of soft, woven *igusa* straw. Walking on it was physiotherapy all unto itself.

Tossing her wrap onto the coat rack, she wanted only to fall facedown on her equally therapeutic traditional Japanese bed and descend into a deep coma. It was a small blessing she had no work tomorrow.

Hopefully, after a day in her pajamas, she'd regain a semblance of the normalcy she'd worked so hard to achieve. A normalcy that seeing Raiden had pulverized all over again.

Crossing the living room on her way to her bedroom, she suddenly stopped when an electrifying sensation skittered up her spine. All her senses went haywire, telling her she wasn't alone. Before they could tell her more, a voice came from behind her, sending her every cell screaming.

"Welcome home, darling."

Three

Her heart lodged into her throat, fright mingling dizzyingly with incredulity, dismay...and exhilaration.

Raiden.

He was here.

Feet away... Inches away... A breath away now.

Every nerve in her body fired in remembrance, in jubilation at the approach of the essence that had once been as familiar to her as her own. For five blazing months of pure passion and pleasure, before she'd had to sever the bond. She'd been bleeding inwardly ever since.

She had no idea how he was here. But from

what she'd learned about him, in her constant search for his news, in her obsessive research of his past, she knew one thing. Raiden could do anything.

As to why he was here, did it matter? It was one more chance to be close to him. A chance that she'd thought she'd never be given again. An unexpected, priceless gift.

That, she knew, was the last thing he wanted to give her. Judging from his tone, dripping in bitter sarcasm and suppressed aggression, he probably wanted to give her five to ten, minimum.

In fact, logically speaking, he should be here to…eliminate her danger. She was the only one who possessed detailed knowledge of the secrets he'd gone to unimaginable lengths to bury. Her existence posed a threat not only to the persona he'd built and the plans he'd worked for since he'd escaped The Organization, but to his very life.

But though he'd assassinated countless people, and she probably deserved to be, in his opinion, she didn't fear for a second that was why he was here. This lethal man with the staggering body count in his past didn't scare her at all.

Not that anything did. With the kind of existence she'd had, she'd never valued her life enough to be afraid for it. The only true fear she'd ever felt had been on his behalf.

"Feet aching, my love?"

Nostalgia skewered through her, made her squeeze her eyes, bite down on the moan that almost escaped her lips.

Welcoming her home, calling her "my darling" and "my love"… They were the same phrases he'd greeted her with that last time in his penthouse in New York five years ago. It had been the first time he'd said things like that…out of bed.

It had been then she'd realized he'd decided to take their relationship to the next level. And that she'd soon be forced to put an end to it.

Unable to face putting a time frame on "soon," that night she'd thrown herself into being with him with all the passion he'd ignited inside her, gulping down every second as if each had been her last ever. But even in her worst nightmares she hadn't expected they would be that for real, that the very next day it would come to such a jarring and dreadful end.

After it had, she'd had no doubt it would remain over.

Then came tonight. Then now. And the bridge into the past she'd thought had burned to ashes had somehow been rebuilt. Because she seemed to have branded him as he'd done her.

He'd already told her that it had been how he'd recognized her in someone else's body. Which flabbergasted her. Even if he'd formed an emotional attachment to her in the past, it had been to the persona she'd played. She'd thought that if he remembered her at all since, it would be with rage and repugnance. She'd never thought he'd obsess over her in any other way.

But by reciting the exact words he'd said that last time they'd met as lovers, he was letting her know he had. From the way he'd drawled the memorized words, he was also letting her know such a hold over him made it more imperative to him to exact revenge for every wrong she'd dealt him, with five years' worth of compound interest.

She would have let him, if it were only she who'd pay the price. But he was in a far more sensitive position than she was. Any impulsive actions would harm him far more than her. And she couldn't let him do this to himself. Not after what she'd done to protect him. She would protect him again, at any cost, even from himself.

It was time to do so, to end this, and this time, make sure it was over for good.

Feeling the heat of his body radiating at her back, tasting the intoxication of his breath as it filled her lungs, she turned slowly, carefully. Her balance was already compromised, and she didn't want to end facedown at his feet instead of on the bed as she'd previously planned.

She almost did so anyway when she laid eyes on him.

Earlier tonight, she'd realized he'd done the impossible, had become even more magnificent than he'd been, his assets having appreciated with maturity, and would no doubt continue to do so. He'd become a god for real, not just in name.

But now... It shouldn't be possible, but he looked even more awe striking than he had an hour ago.

He'd taken off his tuxedo jacket, undid his bow tie and a few shirt buttons, exposing a tantalizing expanse of the burnished flesh beneath. His muscled shoulders and chest seemed wider with just a sheer layer of silk covering them, and in contrast with the now-apparent sparse hardness of his abdomen. And if he looked like this with clothes still on, she didn't want to dwell on the details of his upgrades with them off.

But it was his face that as usual arrested her. His hair was no longer meticulously groomed, the raven-wing, rain-straight locks slightly mussed. It gave him a wild, raw look that made his heart-stopping cheekbones even more prominent, his slanting caramel eyes even more fiery, his sculpted lips more erotic and his chiseled jaw more rugged.

His whole package was enough to compromise her sanity. Not that she'd ever had much to speak of where he was concerned. And that was on the mental and emotional level. On the physical one, just being around him, just thinking of him, made her melt, throb…ache. Her body had been hammering at her, demanding his since she'd laid eyes on him across the ballroom tonight.

His answering appraisal made her core simmer. Then the velvet depths of his baritone drawl almost made it combust.

"Your surgeon didn't only make you a totally different woman, but the most beautiful model possible, too."

She met the eyes that flayed her with contempt with a look of long-perfected equanimity. Even as her insides raged, she injected her voice with the same inexpression.

"Surgeons, in the plural. This result is a collaborative effort, performed over many stages. But it was I who provided them with this 'model.' I needed to be beautiful."

"You were always beautiful."

Her heart forgot a few beats before it resumed sputtering. Outwardly, she knew he'd see no evidence of the effect his words had on her. "Nowhere like this."

"So you thought you needed to intensify your beauty, to boost your effectiveness as a siren? I thought you'd know from intensive experience that outward beauty only lures men, but what traps them are the brains and wiles behind the looks."

"Since I have those, too, I more than ever have

the perfect package." His gorgeous eyes narrowed, his edible lips filled, as if her brazenness aroused him even as it angered him. She pretended to sigh, but really expelled the air that clogged her lungs. "But beauty alone does open doors."

"Doors that might open into untold trouble."

She gave him her best self-assured glance. "True. To inexperienced innocents whose beauty is a bane that makes them a target for exploitation. I, on the other hand, am a seasoned professional who uses my assets as precisely as the situation necessitates. I downplay my looks or even negate them when I want to, and play them to maximum advantage when I need to."

The heat in his eyes rose, even as his expression became arctic. "It must be so freeing, being able to brag about your strategies with someone you've already played. Someone who can't share his insider knowledge with your future victims."

"No bragging involved. Just facts." Before he volleyed a response, she preempted him, turning the focus on him before her heart burst. "Now it's my turn to ask questions."

His lips twisted. "Since you must know everything about me, the only question left in your mind must be how I'm here."

"I do know everything about you," she conceded. "*But* that. So how did you manage to beat me here? And how are you inside my apartment without any sign of breaking and entry? Did you ninja scale your way up here to the thirtieth floor?"

"Contrary to movies, we ninjas don't perform death-defying feats just because we can. We do go for the path of least resistance whenever possible."

"I don't remember ever seeing a ninja bribe a concierge."

"I didn't do that, either." Before she made another comment, he raised his hand, his eyes reflecting his mirthless smile. "I won't tell you how I arrived before you, or how I came in, so save your breath. I'm through sharing secrets with you. And you're finding out no more on your own, either."

She held his gaze. Before she melted into a puddle at his feet, she said, "I bet you didn't sample any of Hiro's first-class sushi or sip his fine *shochu*. I didn't."

His eyes widened at her sharp detour. Before he could adjust, she turned and crossed to her kitchen.

Once there, she looked back over her shoulder. "Seems this is going to be a long night. Want to eat something?"

Raiden watched the one woman he'd been truly intimate with sashay away in that stranger's body.

And his own body roared in unremitting rage...and hunger.

She'd walked away earlier saying, "Forget all about me again." As if he'd ever forgotten about her at all.

But it had been the sane thing to do, to heed her advice. To go back to the ball and his fiancée, to his plans and life, and forget that she existed. Because she in fact never did. Her current identity was just another fictitious figment that would disappear without a trace soon enough, once she'd gotten whatever she was after here. She'd done it once before when he'd been of no further use to her.

But there was nothing sane about what she

made him feel. Never had been, and, it was clear by now, never would be. Renewed exposure to her had caused the fever in his blood to relapse as if it had never subsided at all. As it never had.

The need to have it all out with her ate through his restraint. He'd only ever had speculations about her, didn't have a single fact to quench the maddening thirst to know the truth.

But if he and his brothers had wiped their pasts and created new, perfectly verifiable identities, she'd far surpassed their combined undercover prowess. What they'd done only once, she'd done so many times she seemed to have never had an original identity.

As for their time together, which had scarred him in a way not even his nightmarish existence before it had managed to, he had only theories, no real answers to satisfy the gnawing uncertainty that never stopped asking how. Why?

Now he needed to know the truth.

Though he was certain she'd kept her end of the bargain, since there'd been no hint of suspicion in his identity, he needed to know everything to guard against any breach like hers ever happening again.

Or that was what he'd told himself as he'd torn his way over here. That it was a necessity, a pro-phylactic measure.

Slow steps finally took him to the semi–open plan kitchen. He found her flitting around, her hair up in a wonderfully messy mass.

As soon as he entered, she looked over her shoulder again, nodding toward the island. "Pull up a chair. I won't be long."

He walked up to her instead, struggled not to pull her back against his aching body.

She continued to work with fast, precise move-ments, pausing only when he tucked a lock of hair that had fallen over her shoulder back into her impromptu hairdo.

He bent, murmured in her ear, "Don't you think it weird, with our history, for you to be inviting me to a meal?"

She straightened, continued to work with re-newed zeal. "Why? I invited you to meals be-fore."

And he'd thought everything she'd served him had been ambrosia. "You were someone else then. Actually you weren't someone at all, just a role. One that necessitated satisfying my every hunger to mollify me enough so you could dupe me. Which you did. No more reason for you to feed me."

She flashed him another look over her shoulder that struck his heart like a bolt, before resuming work. "It's the least I can do after I made a fifty-million-dollar-shaped hole in your pocket."

"A fifty-million-dollar meal, eh?" He stepped away before he lost the battle and devoured her instead of the painfully tasty-smelling concoctions she was preparing. He walked back to the island, pulled out a stool and leaned his itching hands on the marble counter. "It had better be *really* good."

"Of course it will be."

There she went again with that supreme assurance. She'd never displayed anything near it in the past.

But then it hadn't been the real her he'd known. She'd been playing the part of the part-time florist and kindergarten teacher who'd been out of her league in his world. In reality, with everything he was, everything he'd seen and done, the reverse might turn out to be true.

She now placed a plate heaped with triple the amount of hers before him, before taking a seat across from him.

He continued watching her, wondering if this was the real her this time, or if it was just another role.

She raised one elegant eyebrow. "You're starving. Eat."

A huff escaped him. She just kept surprising him with every word and action. "And you know that how?"

She pushed the cutlery pointedly at his hands. "Because I calculated that you haven't eaten in at least six hours. I first saw you tonight five hours ago, and you hadn't eaten at least an hour before that. I remember you needed to eat every three hours, with the level of exercise you maintained, and that nuclear metabolism of yours. You seemed to eat almost half my body weight every day. With your increased body mass, you must be in the red by now."

He was. In every way. And he hadn't eaten since breakfast. He'd thought his appetite, which nothing had ever affected except her, had been stalled anticipating the ball. Seemed it had been an advance alarm. He had been anticipating *her.*

She started eating, and he gave in, followed suit.

The moment the thing he was eating hit his taste buds, an involuntary growl of hunger and appreciation rolled from his gut. "What *is* that?"

"Nasu dengaku."

"What?"

Her lips twitched. "You don't know your Japanese cuisine, do you?"

His gaze clung to her lips as her expression filled with what looked like unguarded humor. But it couldn't be. This enigma probably was incapable of spontaneity.

Compressing his lips, he suppressed the moronic impulse to smile back. "I only look Japanese, remember? I spent my first twenty-four years as an identity-less weapon, then when I got out, I became American. I learned everything I could about Japan before I came, but nothing can replace acquiring knowledge firsthand."

She nodded as she chewed, her brilliant eyes doing this hypnotic color dance. "It is a very complex country and culture. Such an extensive mix of modern and traditional, so many regional variations. You'll need at least six months before you're used to the most common daily practices, and a year to comfortably navigate the land and society."

If he didn't know better, he would have thought she was giving him sincere advice to ease his integration into his new homeland. But he did know better.

So what was she doing? No doubt more acting.

The acute senses that had never failed him clamored to detect her duplicity. But she was truly undetectable.

He exhaled. "Are you talking from firsthand experience?"

"I have been here just over a year now." Her gorgeous head inclined, and her deep red silky hair sparked fire in the overhead halogen spotlights. "Bear in mind, it might be years before you can fully integrate. Good news is, speaking fluent Japanese *will* shorten and ease the process. It did for me."

She'd never let on she understood a word of Japanese.

"I have more factors to shorten and ease the

process. I will have a Japanese wife. Something you didn't have."

"I certainly didn't have a Japanese wife."

He held those teasing eyes, and the urge to ask became irresistible. Not one of the dozens of relevant questions, but the one that blocked his throat like a burning coal.

"Is any of this—" he made an encompassing gesture at her "—real? I know your past self was all an act. Is this new persona all a part of your new act?"

Instead of answering with the same directness she had till now, her eyes lowered to her plate as she resumed eating.

He ate, too, because the food was just too delicious and he was famished, and because her silence made him feel as he imagined people did when waiting for a heart-stopping twist in a movie, increasing their popcorn munching in anticipation.

Then she raised her eyes. "I never really acted with you. Apart from the pretense that I was someone…normal, with what that entailed of prefabricated and rehearsed details, everything else—my actions, my characteristics, what I said to you, what I did with you—that was all the real me."

His heart went off like a clap of thunder in his chest.

"Yeah, sure."

She nodded, as if accepting his ridicule. "You asked, and I answered. You're free to take my answer or leave it."

"I'll leave it, if it's all the same to you."

"It is."

He just bet it was.

After wolfing down the last piece of mystery food on his plate, he looked up at her again. "So what was that I just polished off? This *nasu dengaku*?"

"It's grilled aubergine slices marinated in a mix of *hacho-miso* and *shiro-miso* pastes, and covered with ginger and toasted sesame seeds. It's one of my favorite dishes."

"And it just became one of mine." He sat back in his chair. "Anything else to eat? Though it was great, it has nowhere enough calories for my so-called nuclear metabolism."

"Of course. That was just the appetizer."

With that she rose, and went about preparing and serving him two more courses and dessert.

All through, he struggled not to become submerged in the surreal feeling that this was the same woman he'd once wanted with everything in him, that he was sharing with her a warm, intensely enjoyable meal at home. The one thing that kept yanking him out of this false scenario was that he was getting hungrier. For her.

Before that hunger overpowered him, he rose to help her clear the kitchen. After everything had been washed, dried and put away, he turned to her.

"That was unexpected, and unnecessary, and certainly not what I came for. But thanks anyway."

"*That* was appalling." She wrinkled her nose. "You owe me no thanks, and you wouldn't thank me even if I save your life now. But I believe you *were* trying to be gracious, and it only came out the opposite."

"I wasn't aiming at graciousness. As you pointed out, I owe you none."

"But you owed it to your fiancée and Hiro, and you were even worse with them. And that won't work if you want to integrate into Japanese high-class society then take it over. Politeness is paramount here, and the higher you go in society, the more vital it becomes. If you can't *act* gracious with your fiancée and the man holding the ball celebrating your engagement, you're in deep trouble."

"Spoken as the ultimate actress that you are. Maybe I should get lessons from you."

"Maybe you should."

Their gazes collided and wrestled for a long minute.

Before he did what he knew he'd regret, he finally asked the question he'd told himself he'd come here to ask.

"Earlier you said you were sent to expose me as an assassin. Explain."

She gave a dismissing shrug. "What is there to explain?"

"Everything."

"Again? I don't have time for your sweeping generalizations right now. So just narrow down what you want to know, please."

Fighting the urge to roar, he hissed, "Who sent you?"

"Boris Medvedev."

That her response was so immediate, so succinct, would have shocked him all on its own. But that name struck him like a hammer to the temple. It made him stumble back a step.

Medvedev. His personal handler, who'd been assigned to him when he'd been ten. Raiden had spent fourteen horrific years under that man's sadistic eye and lash.

Medvedev had been punished, brutally, when he'd "lost" Raiden. All the handlers had been, when each of his Black Castle brothers had escaped. His brother Rafael had been agonized to know that, as he'd considered his handler, Richard, his mentor. Raiden, however, had been viciously glad that Medvedev had been the most punished and demoted. He owed that man a debt of pain and humiliation nothing could ever satisfy.

But Medvedev wasn't only a sadist, he was an obsessive. It had been what had made Raiden's escape the hardest. And while all their handlers had been sent in search of them, he bet it was Medvedev who'd kept looking after everyone had given up, needing to take his revenge. And most important, to reinstate himself. Though Medvedev had been another abductee of The Organization, he'd suffered from Stockholm syndrome and had integrated totally with his captors. The Organization, and his position within it, was everything to him.

But Raiden had thought even Medvedev had given up the search eventually. He'd underestimated his obsession. And his knowledge of him. His former handler knew him so well he'd suspected his new persona.

But suspicion wouldn't have sufficed. Only solid proof would have been good enough to take to The Organization, that Raiden Kuroshiro, the heavily documented pillar of a global conglomerate like Black Castle Enterprises, was the operative who'd escaped them. Escaped *him.*

So five years ago Medvedev had hired *her,* no doubt the absolute best he could find, to bring him that proof. And she'd found it.

But since Medvedev hadn't made a move since, it was proof she'd upheld her end of the bargain. But now that he knew Medvedev had been her recruiter, he couldn't understand how she had.

He looked at her in renewed confusion. "Medvedev was obsessed with me. He must have watched your every step during those five months, must have demanded regular reports of your progress, and evidence that you were on the right track."

Her eyes turned indigo. "I didn't give him any."

"And he kept financing the fictional life you led? For five months with no signs he might get his money's worth? And it would have been longer if I hadn't discovered you and you were forced to end the charade. Then when you struck your bargain with me, you told him I wasn't the one he thought, and he didn't suspect you'd decided it was more lucrative to work for yourself? Doesn't sound like him."

"I can be very convincing. As you very well know."

With that, it seemed she considered the conversation closed, and she walked past him on her way out of the kitchen. He caught her back to him, slammed her for the second time tonight against his length.

As her breath left her in a gasp that flayed his

chest and neck, his hands tightened on her flesh. "I'm not done here."

Though she was much smaller now without those precarious heels and felt vulnerable in his grip, the entity that held his gaze was the most powerful presence he'd ever encountered.

Then she huskily said, "I am."

"Maybe you are, Scarlett, or Hannah, or whatever your real name is. But *we're* not done."

In one explosive movement fueled by five years of betrayal and frustration, he lifted her up onto the island, yanked up the flowing skirt of her black dress, exposing honey tanned legs and thighs, wrenched them wide apart and slammed between them.

He held her eyes for one last tempestuous moment. They all but screamed at him, *Do it!*

And he did. He lunged, crushed her beneath him, crashed his lips on hers.

Her cry went down his throat as he poured his growls down hers, his lips branding hers, his teeth sinking in their plumpness, his tongue filling her mouth, over and over, invading her, draining her. Her heat and taste and surrender were a sledgehammer to his remaining shell of reason.

His hands glided all over her silkiness, mad with remembrance, sinking in her craved delights, seeking her every memorized trigger, until she writhed beneath him.

At her moan, he slid between her splayed legs down to her core. He nipped her intimate lips through her panties, making her cry out and convulse before he pulled them off with his teeth, his eyes never leaving hers. They'd always told him exactly how she'd felt, what she'd wanted. They'd been far more potent than any mind-altering drug. They still were, sending him clear out of his mind with lust.

She'd always been vocal, too, corroborating her eyes' confessions and demands. Now she said nothing. Yet her body spoke for her, her back arching deeply, legs trembling out of control, core weeping with arousal. She was so ready for him. As she'd always been. He'd always wondered if it had been part of her uncanny ability in subterfuge, if she had a trick to achieve such powerful arousals and orgasms every single time.

But it had felt real then. And it still did. Now she felt as desperate as he was, her body shuddering, her breath fracturing, her skin radiating heat, her core pouring its plea for his possession, its maddening scent perfuming the room, filling his lungs.

He rose between her legs, freeing his rock-hard erection before pushing her knees back against her body, opening her fully for him.

Holding the eyes that had turned into cobalt infernos, without any preliminaries he rammed into her, all his power and pent-up hunger and anger behind the thrust.

Her cry at his abrupt invasion was a red-hot spear in his brain. Like a glove, her slick tightness yielded to his power, sheathed him, searing him with her fever, until he thought she'd burn him to ashes.

For delirious moments, he stilled inside her. This was the ultimate embrace he'd been going insane for. Everything he'd ever craved.

Then the urge to conquer her, to lose himself inside her crested again, and he withdrew, then plunged again and again, harder each time, faster. Her cries punctuated his thrusts. Every time he sank deeper, the need to breach her, to bury himself into her recesses, blinded him.

He lodged inside her to the root, and she arched in a deep bow, her inner muscles clamping his hardness in unbearable tautness, her face clenching in agonized urgency, her every muscle beneath and around him buzzing on the edge of a paroxysm. Another thrust would make her explode in release.

He gave it to her, with everything in him.

Her shriek pierced him as her core splintered around his girth and his body all but detonated in the most powerful orgasm he'd ever experienced, even with her. His roars echoed her desperation as his body caught the current of her convulsions. Excruciating pleasure shot through his length in jet after jet of white-hot release until he felt he'd drained his essence into her depths.

The world seemed to vanish as he slumped on top of her, nothing left but feeling her beneath him, still trembling, her core still milking him for every last drop of sensation.

In what could have been an hour, the arms and legs that lay nerveless with satiation around him started to tighten, as did the velvet gripping his erection.

She wanted more. She always had. Once had never been enough for her. Or for him. With her, he'd always wanted more, longer, harder, over and over.

Feeling disgusted with himself, he pulled out of her depths, yanked himself from her clinging limbs.

As soon as he stood up, she slipped off the counter, and the dress he'd only pushed out of the way to take her now tumbled down to cover her seminakedness. In seconds she looked as if nothing had happened.

Tearing his gaze away, he tugged his zipper closed and stuffed his shirt back into his pants in suppressed violence before he strode out to the living room to pick up his jacket.

At the door, he turned, found her standing in the distance, the face that had been gripped in feverish passion just minutes earlier a mask of inanimate beauty.

Flicking her one last contemptuous glance, he said, "Now we're done."

Four

Scarlett felt done in, done for. Just done.

As Raiden had said they were.

Last night, his explosive lovemaking—what she'd been yearning for for five interminable years—had inundated her with the physical satisfaction only he had ever given her. But she'd wanted more, far more. A whole night in his arms. A night of worshipping him and giving herself to him in the intimacy she'd only ever had with him, could never have with another. She'd wanted a new intense memory of him to help keep the frozen wasteland inside her from claiming the last flickering flame of life. What had sprung into existence in the first place because of him.

Keeping obsessive track of his news in the past years had been the one thing that had kept that flame from being extinguished. As long as he'd been safe and soaring from one success to a higher one, it had been enough to keep her going.

Then he'd taken her, what she'd never even dared dream would ever happen again. And as he'd filled her arms and body, his eyes burning her with his ferocious hunger, an insane hope had ignited among the hopelessness she'd been resigned to all her life. That she might have him again, without the need to hide anything from him, for a whole night. More, if he would allow it.

But that wasn't what it had been about for him.

He'd needed to get this, and her, out of his system. He'd needed the closure. Now that he had it, he'd finally move on. As she wanted him to. She'd never wanted anything but his peace.

But the way he'd ended the delirious interlude—with disgust, clearly at himself more than her…

Her phone rang. She grabbed for it, thankful for the distraction. It was Hiro. After he'd once kept insisting she was his hero, she'd laughingly told him she'd make his ringtone "I Need a Hero." She had.

Affection welled inside her, played on lips still stiff with Raiden's rejection as she hit Answer.

"I kissed Megumi."

After a moment's surprise at Hiro's blurted confession, she chuckled. "And I thought I'd be apologizing for leaving last night without telling you. Seems I did you a favor. The moment I left your side, you pursued your fantasy woman, got her alone and did what you should have done long ago."

"It's no laughing matter, Scarlett." Hiro sounded as if he'd suffer a heart attack any second now.

It never ceased to amaze her how the ruthless financial mogul could be so different on a personal level. With her, he had a center made of marshmallow. But when it came to Megumi, his insides were clearly more the consistency of Jell-O.

Not that anyone would believe it. The Japanese weren't given to expressing their emotions, even with their closest people. It was probably because she was a gaijin and a friend who had no contact with his close circle that Hiro felt safe to show her a side of him he'd never show his compatriots and kin. Of course, there was also that life-changing experience he'd shared with her, making her closer to him than almost everyone. Certainly closer than the woman of his dreams, whom he'd finally taken a step toward. If a very belated one.

Scarlett didn't understand why he'd never taken it before. He'd tell her why if and when he saw fit. Or not. She'd be there for him, as he was for her, no questions asked.

"I broke my code of honor. I compromised hers, showed her disrespect and exploited Kuroshiro's trust in accepting my tribute and bringing her to my home. It was a total disaster."

Hiro's deep voice was strangled, choking off the measure of joy his call had given her. He was really taking this badly, was calling to share his self-recriminations because they'd become too much for him to bear alone.

She wished she could tell him he should at least feel no remorse on Raiden's behalf. He had not only kissed *her* but had sex with her. But though Raiden was a major concern to him, what so agonized him was what he thought he'd done to Megumi.

Deciding to go for the heart of the matter, she asked, "Did she respond?"

That seemed to surprise him so much, it aborted his agitation, made him sound scandalized as he said, "Is that all you have to say? What's the difference if she did?"

"It makes all the difference. So did she?" Only his deep, disturbed breathing answered her. "Let me put it another way. Did she resist you?"

A heavy exhalation. "No. She melted in my embrace, as I always dreamed she would, gave me her lips to worship." An exasperated exhalation. "But that was no response."

She groaned. "Hiro, Hiro, don't you know anything about women at all? That *was* her response. Surrendering to you, letting you claim her as you will."

She'd done the same with Raiden. Heat surged through her with the memories of what Raiden had done to her, the unimaginable pleasure he'd given her when he'd taken her like that, devoured her without preliminaries, as if he couldn't wait, couldn't breathe if he didn't have her. It had always been intoxicating when she'd met him kiss for kiss, touch for touch, taken what she'd wanted, which had always been all of him. But her utmost pleasure had always been to submit to his dominance, as she had last night.

"But afterward, she looked…shocked."

She barely held back from moaning with the pangs of renewed hunger as she focused on her distressed friend. "Of course she did. You've never shown her signs you have emotions for her, then suddenly at her engagement party, you drag her aside and devour her."

"I did show her my emotions," Hiro protested. "Every time I saw her for the past six months. But my father was Yakuza, and I thought that might be why she'd never consider me."

That was the first time Hiro admitted his late father had been a member of the Japanese mafia, and she wouldn't probe further. "Did you make any actual advances before last night?"

"I invented ways to see her as frequently as I can."

"Did she realize that? Or did you hide your

intentions so well, like you did last night, she didn't realize you set those events up with the sole purpose of seeing her?"

"She moves in completely different circles to mine, so I joined every society and charity she works with, when they're completely unrelated to my interests. She must have realized I only did that to see her. And I paid only her compliments. I also mentioned many times how I thought it was the perfect time to marry. It seemed she enjoyed my interest, encouraged it, and I was working up the nerve to go to her father with my proposal. Then a week ago, her engagement to Kuroshiro was announced, a man she met only days before. A man her father approves of."

So this was how recent this whole arrangement was.

She exhaled. "Listen, Hiro, the young woman I saw last night felt uncertain of herself in spite of her incredible beauty. She probably couldn't believe a man like you was interested in her. Maybe she needed a direct approach, not all those elaborate hints. I can tell you for sure that she was seriously agitated when you took me to her and…Mr. Kuroshiro."

"She didn't look agitated." His frown was clear in his tone.

"That goes to show you that you can't read her, and probably missed all the signs of her reciprocating interest. For she was certainly agitated, and it was because of you." She exhaled. "Seems this was a case of tragic miscommunication."

"And now it's too late," Hiro groaned. "I should have sought your counsel before and all this might have not happened. Now I've made it so much worse by kissing her. I'd hoped to continue to see her in a social setting, but now I won't be able to see her again at all. I've truly lost her."

Before she protested that he hadn't, she remembered.

This was the woman Raiden would marry in ten weeks. Raiden *needed* to marry her, for a reason no one but she knew. And he wouldn't let anyone stand in his way. It was better for Hiro to forget about Megumi. For she *was* already lost to him.

She wished she could reach out through the phone and hug him. They had even more in common than she'd thought, wanting the one person they could never have. The irony was the two people they wanted would marry each other. But he was in an even worse situation, because he'd always pine for Megumi, think he might have had her if only he'd acted differently. She, on the other hand, had never entertained the possibility that she could have Raiden. The certainty of despair was better than agonizing what-ifs.

"I'm so sorry, Hiro." She groaned her pain on his behalf. "But if this is any consolation, I do believe Megumi reciprocated your feelings. From what I saw last night, I believe she would have chosen you if she could. I also don't think you compromised her honor or disrespected her when you kissed her. You simply let her know you wanted her for her, not for her family connections. That's a knowledge she'll treasure for the rest of her life."

After that, Hiro abruptly changed the subject, as if he couldn't bear talking about Megumi anymore but was too polite to just end the call. She did it for him, excusing herself to finish up her work. From the way he sounded as he said goodbye, it seemed she'd said all the right things to defuse his distress—only to substitute it with despondence.

But he would have gotten there on his own. Losing the only one you want was the most crushing experience one could suffer. She knew. For she'd had too many horrific experiences, and nothing had hit her harder than losing Raiden.

And there was nothing she could do about it. Not then, not now.

But she could do something about the report she was working on. She had to wrap up this last stage in her project, then she could leave Japan. After what had happened with Raiden, she couldn't stay any longer. It had been one thing to be in the same country as him, to know he was getting married, even see him from afar, when she'd thought he'd never recognize her. But now that he had, now that he'd reignited her, she couldn't bear to see him again if even by chance. She'd miss seeing Hiro regularly like crazy, but losing his constant presence in her life was a price she had to pay.

Right now, she had to finish setting up the

shelters in Kyoto. She'd no longer stay to oversee them as she'd planned, so she had to have a system in place to make up for her absence.

To think of all the effort she'd done after she'd joined UNICEF, to come to Japan especially to set up branches of the aid organization in Tokyo. She'd long finished setting up the executive headquarters in downtown Tokyo, orchestrating relief, relocation and disaster-counseling services. She'd since been working on a few locations across Japan for shelters and rehabilitation centers for the children who'd lost family and survived trauma related to man-made crises and natural disasters, especially the most recent earthquake and tsunami. Now she'd have to drop everything and leave when she'd thought she'd stay for years to come. Her time here would be weeks at most now. Days if she could manage it.

Then she'd never be in danger of seeing Raiden again.

This time, it would be truly over.

Raiden stood gazing unseeingly from the window of his new headquarters overlooking downtown Tokyo, again trying to bring his rioting senses under control. And again he failed.

His fury was completely directed at himself. This time, she had nothing to do with any of it. It had been his fault alone that he'd succumbed to this sick need for her. Even knowing exactly what she was, or worse, not knowing anything about her, only that everything about her was a lie. And now he couldn't stop reliving every blazing moment of his possession of her.

One thing he had to admit: they were not done.

Having her once wasn't enough. He needed more. Had to have it. It was imperative he got her out of his system. And this wouldn't happen by walking away and trying to clobber that need into submission. It had been consuming him for five years, but after that maddening taste of her, the fire would only rage higher, burn his sanity to ashes faster.

There was one way this could end. If he gave in to his lust to the very end, bingeing on her until he was glutted.

And he had to do it now. He needed everything resolved before his wedding. He wasn't letting anything jeopardize his plans, starting with his own weakness. Everything he'd worked for the past ten years was at stake.

That was how long he'd been looking for his bloodline. Since his escape from The Organization. Not that he'd been doing nothing but. Since then he'd joined his brothers who'd escaped before him, and they'd set up Black Castle Enterprises together. It had taken some doing adjusting his literally deadly ninja methods to a figurative level in business. But searching for his family had remained a major concern. The one time he'd totally forgotten about his quest had been when he'd been with her in the past.

Finally, a couple of months back, with the benefit of years of research and his brothers' help, especially the last bit of analysis Rafael Salazar had provided, he'd finally reconstructed who he was and how he'd been taken by The Organization.

But though The Organization itself had had no idea who his family was, he still couldn't let his family know that he was their long-lost relative. He was certain The Organization had never shelved his case and might put two and two together if his origins were made public. A child lost in a tsunami returning to such a well-known family as the Hashimotos as such a high-profile adult would no doubt trigger correct deductions.

He'd already had a brush with exposure five years ago. With Hannah...or Scarlett. Now that he knew it had been Medvedev on his trail, and she'd thrown him off once, it was more imperative than ever he maintained his secrecy, or risk arousing that monster's suspicions again.

And he also couldn't risk his newfound family finding his origins. The Hashimotos were among a handful of families in Japan that were second only to the imperial family in lineage, their bloodline reaching back over a thousand years into Japan's history. If they found out anything of his past, they'd reject him irrevocably. They wouldn't care that it hadn't been of his choosing. They had only samurai in their lineage. Ninjas were anathema to them.

But all his life he'd dreamed of reclaiming his family name, of taking his rightful place at its head and in Japanese society, upholding the traditions he'd been meant to, if not for the disaster that had robbed him of his family and left him prey to those who'd exploited him for twenty years. Nothing would prevent him from reaching his goal now.

But since it was out of the question letting his family know he was his father's heir and the rightful head of the family, he'd concocted another plan that would secure his goals without divulging his real identity.

That plan had come to him while researching Japanese society. He'd found out that adult adoptions were the most prevalent form of adoption in Japan, especially with the son-in-law taking his wife's family name and becoming their heir. Since his father's second cousin, Takeo Hashimoto—now the head of the family—had one unmarried daughter, he'd decided to marry her, and through *yōshi-engumi,* literally "marriage and adoption," become a *mukoyōshi,* an adopted husband.

He'd put his plan in motion a month ago, coming to Japan to dangle himself in front of Takeo, a tycoon any family would do anything to have as *mukoyōshi,* providing the strongest heir possible and taking the family's position and power to new levels. He'd been certain his uncle would make an offer. And he had. He'd offered

Megumi, the family name and leadership and the helm of its current businesses.

After pretending to refuse, then to need persuasion, Raiden had accepted. And he was finally weeks away from reclaiming all he'd lost, everything that was rightfully his.

The one thing in the way now was his obsession with Scarlett. There was no other option but to get rid of it.

In an hour, he was sitting in the back of his limo, his American driver-cum-head bodyguard standing outside for a smoke. He allowed it only since he couldn't smell him through the airtight partition. And because Steve was the best.

Nothing on his level, of course. But the best in the private security world.

Suddenly he sat up, his senses on alert. The next second, he saw her step out of the building they were parked in front of.

He'd again felt her before he'd seen her.

Scarlett saw him the moment he saw her, stopped.

Holding her gaze across the distance, he threw the door open. "Get in."

After a moment of stillness, she walked to the limo, her steps graceful, tranquil. The crowds going and coming on the pavement parted for her, everyone turning to look in fascination at the gaijin woman who looked like a living splash of color among the mostly two-tone population.

When she reached the limo, he slid across the backseat, making space for her, and watched greedily as she lowered her lush, elegant body beside him. Her heat and scent enveloped him, made hunger writhe inside him.

She looked different today, yet another woman. Nothing like last night's femme fatale. A working woman with practical clothes, a scrubbed-clean face and a prim ponytail. She could have been wearing the most outrageous lingerie or even been naked and on erotic display from the way his hormones hurtled in scalding torrents in his arteries.

He sat back and looked away before he dragged her over him or lunged and crushed her beneath him. Steve came in at once and, raising the opaque, soundproof partition between them, put the car in motion as per Raiden's earlier orders.

After a minute when she sat staring ahead and

silent beside him, he said, "I have an offer for you."

"I'm listening." The way she said the words, calm yet immediate, told him she couldn't wait to hear his offer.

He couldn't wait to make it, either. "I want you in my bed, every night, starting tonight. Until I get married. You can ask for whatever *you* want and its yours."

Silence stretched between them after his succinct proposition.

Then she finally turned to him, drawing him to face her as if by sheer magnetism.

Her eyes emitted blue, hot fire in the limo's semidarkness, the one-way-mirror windows dimming the bright lights of the city. What he could see of her expression was enigmatic. "Don't you think a flare of passion is one thing, but an affair is another?"

He shrugged. "It's not an affair. It's an arrangement. A purely sexual one."

Her lashes lowered for moments, before rising. "What about your engagement? Your fiancée?"

"Megumi only wants to honor her family by marrying the most influential man, producing heirs carrying his genes and accessing his power and wealth. She, like me, expects our lives to remain separate, with intimacies practiced only to acquire said heirs."

"So have you started…practicing yet?"

He frowned. After the intimacies with her, the very idea filled him with outright revulsion.

He gritted down on the unwilling reaction. "Of course not. You don't need to worry I'd come to you from her or another woman's bed. As in the past, while I'm with you, I will be with you alone." A vicious doubt twisted in his gut. "I don't know what you did back then, but I expect the same finite monogamy from you now."

"I was with no one else."

And somehow, even though he now knew she seduced men for a living, he believed her.

Silence stretched again until he wanted to grab her and demand she tell him what she was thinking. Now that he knew she'd tell him, the urge to know her every thought almost overpowered him. He held back, reminding himself everything he felt was a by-product of intense lust. Once that was satisfied, curiosity, possessiveness and everything else would subside with it.

He inhaled. "Now give me your pledge that you will be at my disposal for the next ten weeks."

At his terse command, her gaze clashed with his in mock surprise. "You mean you'd believe my 'pledge'?" At his curt nod, she exhaled. "And I can ask for anything I want you say?"

"Anything."

"Even if I ask for another fifty million dollars?"

"Yes."

If she had any doubt how much he wanted her, she should have no doubt now. He didn't mind letting her know. For the duration of the arrangement, he was giving in to his every urge, saying and doing everything that came to him the moment it did, no control, no premeditation. He'd plunge whole into this with her. It was the only way he'd purge her from his system, the only way he'd ever emerge whole.

For good measure, he added, "I will pay the whole amount up-front."

Her gaze was more unreadable as she tilted her head at him. "How can you, the ruthless financier that you are, pay that exorbitant amount up-front? How do you know I won't just take the money and disappear like I did in the past?"

"I know for two reasons. The first is that you did uphold your pledge to me once. You do seem to possess a code of some sort. The second and more important reason is because you won't want to. I was there last night, remember? You were as starving for me as I was for you. I might despise you, might believe everything between us had been a lie, but I know the physical side was real."

"You do?"

Her soft provocation hit him like an ax, snapping the last tethers of control. He gave in, dragged her over his lap, pressed her down on his steel erection.

Grinding up into her, drawing an involuntary moan from her and an answering grind, he touched his open lips to her pulse point. "Yes, I know. I know that I was the best you ever had. That you haven't found anything near what we shared. That after last night, you're burning for more."

Holding him in her hypnotic gaze, she nodded, silently conceding everything he'd said.

Then in a low, raw whisper, she said, "Then give me more, Raiden. Now."

"Yes." The word escaped him on a scalding hiss as he freed himself. Then he bunched her skirt up before lifting her up to hover over his thick crown. His hands fisted at her hips as he tore her panties away, making her gasp.

His erection thudded against her molten lips, making her fingers dig in his shoulders. "Now, Raiden. *Now.*"

Everything in him surged at her tremulous urgency, tensed when she wrapped her fingers around him and positioned him at her soaking entrance, tried to bear down on him.

She was as tight as ever, what had always made him think he wouldn't fit inside her. But their almost impossible fit had always made them incoherent with pleasure, driven them to pinnacles of wild satisfaction. It had again last night. It would always do so. The scent of their lust rose heavy and humid in the limo as he began invading her.

"So ready." He groaned at the delicious agony as she opened to him, singed him with her heat and honey. "So right."

Her eyes squeezed shut and she moaned as he forged into her clenching depths, stretching her beyond her capacity.

Pressing her lower belly, he slid his thumb between her drenched folds, rubbed her nub in slow circles, and she cried out, clenched tighter around his girth, taking him deeper. She opened her lust-heavy eyes and watched him feverishly.

She was so beautiful draped over him like that, her lithe body straining against and around his, needing his occupation, his pleasuring. He already felt she'd always look like that. To him, she'd always be *her,* the one woman he craved, no matter what she looked like, or what she was.

"Perfect," he bit out, his teeth grinding with the avalanche of sensations as he began to thrust up into her. "Always perfect."

Her heat rose with his praise, and she became even wetter, letting him slide smoothly farther inside her.

"So hot and hard, so deep… You're so deep inside me. Take me, Raiden, do it to me, all the way inside me…*Raiden*…" she keened, over and over, fidgeting around him to ease the edge of pain she'd confessed always accompanied his complete occupation. But he also knew it made her pleasure sharper, her release more explosive. Her body was corroborating his knowledge, rippling around him, squeezing, trembling on the verge of orgasm. And he hadn't fully sheathed himself inside her yet. He was hovering on the edge, too.

Cursing, he knew they were too inflamed, would combust too quickly. But he was damned if he'd let them come without being inside her all the way, as she demanded, as he needed.

Gripping her hips, he leaned her backward, altering the angle of her descent, making her open fully for his plundering. A breathless cry escaped her as she took him to the root.

After waiting out the blinding sensation of being buried inside her to the hilt, he withdrew, dragging a soft shriek from her depths, along with his erection. He thrust back. And she screamed, came all over him, her body lurching in convulsions, inside and out. He rode her harder as she came, his grasp on her hips ferocious. Pleasure spread from where they connected to every inch of his body as he felt her finish, then without pause start to climb again up the spiral of carnal desperation.

"Please…" She lurched forward to press her gasping mouth to his, her fingers gripping his sweat-dampened hair as she rode him, begging him with body and trembling pleas to end her renewed torment. "I'm coming again. Raiden, please, come with me…."

He lost his mind, the need to finish her and empty himself into her taking over completely. Tilting her, he angled his thrusts, pummeling against that trigger inside her. She at once tightened and shook, then exploded into another shrieking orgasm. Grabbing her by the nape, he fed her convulsions, his hips becoming a blur as he pounded into her, making her writhe and moan and come harder, her body heaving with every discharge of pleasure.

"Hannah!" His bellow of ecstasy sounded feral in his own ears as at last his orgasm tore into him, his seed scorching through his length and shooting into her milking depths in jet after agonizingly pleasurable jet.

Their mutual release raged on until he was fully drained and she collapsed on top of him, a boneless mass of tremors and satiation. She pressed her face to his equally hot, moist neck, her breath gusting to the same labored rhythm as his.

The limo undulated smoothly through the streets of Tokyo as they lay there, like last night, both fully clothed, only merged at their most intimate parts, which made it all more excruciatingly erotic. He finally brushed his lips across hers, as if comforting her in the aftermath of this mind-blowing interlude, what he again hadn't expected or planned.

"Call me Scarlett." Her whisper hit his cheek with her still-gasping breaths.

"Is that your real name?"

"No. But it…has meaning to me."

What was that? And what was her real name? Where did she come from? Would she ever tell him? Should he demand to know?

No. Their relationship would remain at this sexual level, would never go any further. He'd once thought it could, would, but he'd been wrong. Now there was no place in his life for anything but his plans. And even without his plans, he had no place in his life for someone like her. He was sure she had none for him, either.

He carefully disengaged their bodies, even though he was already clamoring for round two, and tidied them both up.

In minutes, she was once again sitting beside him, looking so deceptively prim in her utilitarian clothes and ponytail, as if she hadn't just combusted in his arms and wrung a new level of ecstasy from his every cell. He brushed damp tendrils of hair off her temples, cupped her cheek.

When she shuddered and pressed her flesh harder into his palm, his lips crooked in a smile. "I trust that was to your satisfaction?"

Her eyes went black. "To my ecstasy. Now I want more."

Pride revved inside his chest. For he was certain she meant it. She couldn't wait to have him again. Even if he didn't already know that, she had no reason to exaggerate. He'd already offered her everything she might want up front.

"You only have to give me your word and you'll have ten weeks' worth of more. With a huge cash incentive. To put things in perspective."

Her eyes grew opaque, making him regret those last words. Before he found a way to take them back, she finally nodded.

But before relief surged, she added, "But since it's for a good cause, how about doubling that cash incentive to a hundred million dollars?"

Five

"Are you mourning parting with your nine-figure sum?"

Scarlett bent over the couch and slid her arms over Raiden's seminaked body as she whispered the teasing question into his ear.

He remained unmoving, staring ahead through the floor-to-ceiling window at the spectacular Tokyo Bay at sunset.

Which was weird. For the past three weeks since they'd started their...arrangement, he'd always met her halfway as soon as she'd entered, always impatient, urgent, voracious.

It had become her nightly ritual, and whenever possible a midday one, too, coming to his penthouse, to which he'd given her full access. He'd gotten this apartment in the first place for her, acquiring it the very next day after she'd agreed to his proposition, to be a few blocks away from her apartment. This, and everything else he did continued to be in the service of her convenience, and to make the most time for each other, wasting as little as possible commuting.

Before she came here every evening, she passed by her place and prepared an overnight bag. When she departed before his housekeepers came, she left no evidence behind to betray that Raiden shared this place with a woman.

She also went home first to shower. *He* showered as soon as he returned home and was always starving for her at the end of his workday, and she couldn't let him take her to bed fresh, or not so fresh, from hers. She'd been flying back and forth daily to the areas still affected by the last earthquake and tsunami in the northeast of Honshu island, and the fieldwork she'd been doing had been grueling. Over three hundred thousand people were still in temporary housing, and over ten thousand of those were orphaned children, the focus of her work. She'd been going all out setting up their special shelters. She needed to get things up and running before she left.

Her departure had become even more imperative now. The day, the *hour* her time with Raiden was up, she'd leave Japan and never come back.

Till then she'd spend every possible second with him. And Raiden was beyond generous with his time. Her days, as per his decree, were hers—*if* he couldn't get away and meet her back here. Her nights were all his. She was so very okay with that.

Then in the mornings they left separately, and they never met anywhere else. There were no lunches or dinners or evenings out. They'd been taking every precaution to make sure their arrangement remained a secret. She was even more careful than he was. When she left this time, she wanted to leave him nothing but good memories, and no lasting damage of any sort.

That was, nothing more than the hundred-million-dollar-shaped new hole in his pocket.

It still flabbergasted her that he could so easily part with that much money. But he had, without batting an eyelash. Right there in his limo, he'd just produced his checkbook from his hand-tailored jacket, and had written the check. Payable the very next day.

At her incredulity that he'd done that when she didn't have the blade of exposure held to his neck this time, he'd shrugged, saying he considered having her those ten weeks as vital to him as keeping his secrets had been. She'd insisted he hadn't needed to give her anything, that what she wanted was only him. And he'd only said he knew that.

But he'd still been ready to part with such a staggering sum. To put things into perspective. So she wouldn't mistake this for anything permanent.

She could have told him there'd never been any danger of that.

But she didn't tell him. Nor did she talk about anything else of note, either. Their time together was about indulging in each other. Ten weeks of pure pleasure.

Not that she thought it would be really that long. There was no way he'd be with her right up to his wedding day.

Swallowing the lump she had no right to have

perpetually in her throat, she ran her palms over his chest and abdomen, luxuriating in his velvet-encased steel flesh, tracing every bulge and ridge and groove of his chiseled perfection.

Then she went lower, afraid she'd find more evidence of disinterest to go with his unprecedented preoccupation, and her breath left her in a ragged sigh as her hand closed over his mind-blowing potency, fully, dauntingly aroused.

Her lips shaking in relief, she bit his earlobe as she squeezed him. "I need you to be doing far better things than staring out into the horizon like that. Like taking me right here, right now."

"Scarlett."

That was all he said as he flung his head against the back of the couch, exposing his face and neck to her worship.

But he hadn't moaned her name in pleasure, or in sensual threat. But as if he was...trying to understand it.

Suddenly the whole world turned upside down. He'd grabbed her and flipped her in the air, bringing her down across his body.

Breathless with shock and with awe at his sheer strength and prowess, she gaped up at him.

It had been effortless for him to catapult her like this. His hands hadn't dug hard in her flesh to secure her, then he'd applied what felt like antigravity to her descent in midflip so that she landed with the softest of impacts on his lap.

Sealing her open mouth with a kiss that breached her essence, he finally withdrew to look down at her as she lay cradled in his arms, nerveless still with surprise and sheer delight. She would have stayed like this forever if she could.

He lifted a thick lock of her long hair to his lips before winding it around his hand, giving a tug that sent a million delicious arrows shooting everywhere through her body.

One of her various addictions to him was to how he gave her pleasure with every touch, every action. But when he plundered her, he had her screaming with it, tethering her by her hair, harnessing her to make her submit to his every demand. It bordered on savagery, and was pure perfection.

She wished she could ask him to grow his magnificent hair longer, so she could grab it as she held on to him, as he pounded into her, drove her beyond her limits and herself and the world.

But she had no right to ask anything of him, even if his indulgence of her knew no bounds. And even if she did ask, and he didn't have to keep it cropped for his image and grew it out, she wouldn't be around long enough to enjoy the results.

Megumi would. She knew he believed his fi-ancée would endure intimacy with him only for the purpose of making their required heirs, but Scarlett believed any woman he touched would crave him forever afterward. As she did.

"It's too obvious," he suddenly said. "To pick Scarlett because you chose to be a redhead in this incarnation."

It was as if he was continuing a conversation he'd been having with himself. Was that why he'd been lost in thought? Searching for explanations as to why she'd chosen that name?

He'd had questions sometimes, what would have led to discussing her past and dissecting it. She'd diverted him every time. But he kept going back to her name, the one she'd chosen for her latest, and she hoped, last identity. It was as if he was trying to grab the end of a thread that would help him unravel her mystery. A person's given name might not say much about them, but a chosen one said a lot, could be a clue that would lead to their truth. What she never wanted him, of all people, to find out.

But instead of evading the question again, she decided to give him a measure of truth. "I did choose the name because it would make people think my parents picked the obvious name for a redhead. But it's just a coincidence, since it has personal significance to me, what no one else would ever figure out."

His focus became absolute. "What is that?"

She gave him another piece. "It reminds me of my mother."

His eyes smoldered. "Did you lose her long ago?"

"Over twenty years ago."

He frowned. "You must have been too young to remember her."

"I was old enough to remember everything."

His gaze grew more probing. "I wouldn't give you more than twenty-five or -six."

"I'm older than I look."

She was actually almost twenty-nine, had been seven when she'd lost her mother. Or rather, when *she* had been lost to her mother.

But she wouldn't pinpoint her age. She drew the line at giving him specifics. But she'd appease his curiosity with one more truth.

"The first fairy tale my mother ever told me at night was *Little Red Riding Hood.* It remained my favorite bedtime story. But since I couldn't have named myself Red, I went for Scarlett."

As soon as her lips stilled, he bent and took them in a long, drugging kiss. As if rewarding her for satisfying one of his curiosities about her.

Pulling back, she noticed a touch of something she hadn't seen since they'd met again, but had seen a lot five years ago when he'd thought she'd been the fictitious Hannah McPherson, the normal woman who'd lost her parents as he had. Empathy. Even tenderness.

Could she be imagining it? She shouldn't.

"I was two when I lost my parents. But you know that already."

She nodded, her throat tightening as she imagined the lost boy he'd been. She realized it was the first time he'd talked about it. She'd never thought he would share any of his scars with her.

He started sweeping her from head to hip in caresses as he talked, his gaze fixed on her eyes but seemingly looking into his own memories. "In the two years I spent in the shelter, no one ever told me that my parents were dead. They probably thought I was too young to understand what that meant, or they weren't really sure they were. There were thousands still missing and unaccounted for."

Like after the last and most powerful earthquake and tsunami to hit Japan. Years later, over twenty-one thousand people were still missing.

"After The Organization took me when I was four, it took a long while to understand I was imprisoned and that I'd never see my family again, the family I barely remembered anymore. It was twenty years later that I managed to escape."

Unable to hold back, she pulled him down to her and sealed his lips with her own, as if she could absorb his remembered pain and abuse.

Letting her drink deep of his essence, he swept her around to bring her beneath him on the gigantic couch. He stretched over her, his daunting hardness pressing where she needed it through their clothes. He was clad only in black pants. The rest of his body was a poem of defined, elegant muscles, packing unimaginable power, flexing and straining their hunger over her. How she'd soon have to live without this unbridled joy of feeling him like this, she couldn't begin to think. She'd done it once before, falling into the suspended animation that had been the only way she could survive. She had no idea if she'd be able to seek its refuge again.

Her heart thudded painfully as Raiden pulled back from their kiss and started to rise. Unable to let him go, she clung to his arms. He let her, surrendering to her caresses like a great feline inviting and luxuriating in a worshipper's petting.

Then his eyes took on that reminiscing cast again. "I was always angry that I didn't even remember my family. I wished I had been older when I lost them so I'd at least have the memories. It made it so much harder finding their trail." His gaze focused back on her, that gentleness entering it again. "But just now as you said you remembered everything about your mother,

I realized that I got the better deal. Memories are far more painful than their absence."

Feeling her throat closing over what felt like barbs, she struggled to keep her eyes from filling with tears.

Before she lost the fight, he speared his hand in her hair at her nape, pinning her head down to the couch, tilting her face up to him. "So you're not a real redhead, either."

"No."

His other hand threaded through her hair, combing it over and over. "You made a very convincing blonde, too. Any shade suits you so much it looks as if you were born with it. Until you try the next shade and it's just as incredible on you."

She stored away the praise he lavished on her, saving it for the barren years ahead. Even if it was mostly about her looks, which weren't hers anyway anymore, she would hold on to it.

She shrugged. "Blond colors were the best to turn into others at short notice. Now that I have no need for changing colors, I can maintain a darker one."

"But now that you don't need to change colors, why not just go back to your original one? Wouldn't that be more convenient? Or do you like how this shade makes you stand out here?"

She couldn't tell him she continued dying her hair obsessively because she couldn't bear seeing the thick white lock that had grown in her crown after she'd left him. A glaring souvenir of the most mutilating period of her life.

So she told him the reason she'd chosen this shade instead. "This was actually my paternal aunt's hair color. I loved her so much, thought she looked like a fairy queen with that hair. And I made my face look like a childhood friend. At least, what I think she would have looked like as an adult."

"Are your aunt and friend dead, too?" At her difficult nod, the empathy she thought she saw in his gaze grew contemplative. "So you've created this new identity from the memories of the people you loved and lost, becoming a living memorial of them."

Surprise at his analysis made her lose the fight, hot, stinging tears rushing to her eyes.

Averting them, she whispered, "I never looked at it this way. It just comforted me to look in the mirror and see a reflection of the ones I loved, to hear the name that reminds me of my mother's soft voice telling me stories in the dark."

Bringing her eyes back to his with a gentle hand on her cheek, his fingers wiped away the tears that had escaped, his gaze lengthening, deepening, until she felt he'd fathomed her every secret without her needing to tell him any more details.

Suddenly he asked, "How many disguises did you have in your life?"

Blinking to clear her eyes, she attempted a mischievous smile. "Aren't you all questions to-night?"

His answering smile was equal parts hunger and self-deprecation. "You fascinate me. I thought I was undetectable until you. I'd give anything to pick your brains."

"Anything?" She ran a finger down his chest, then the groove separating his defined abs, then lower.

"Name your price."

"Any price?"

He just nodded, his expression avid, his irises

looking as if they had the sunset at his back trapped in them.

God, how could anything be so absolutely beautiful?

Sighing, she arched up into his length, ran greedy hands down his muscled back. "You know my price."

"That's not a price, that's a privilege. One I'll take full advantage of, as soon as you quench my curiosity. So how many?"

"How many personas have I played, you mean? Many."

"I'm sure you have an exact number."

"Sixty-seven."

His eyes snapped wider. He must have expected her to prevaricate, and probably couldn't imagine someone could have played that many roles.

At length, he said, "Counting the two personas I know?"

"No."

At her immediate answer, he pursed his lips. "Why not? They are very well-drawn and distinct personas."

"Just in their different names and life stories."

"Still claiming you never acted with me?"

"You be the judge of that." She took one of his hands, guided it beneath her panties. As his fingers slid between her swollen, melting flesh, his erection grew so hard, it hurt poking into her side. "Can this be an act?"

"Not this, for sure."

Moaning, she opened herself to him, and those long, powerful fingers caressed her feminine lips apart, sawed through her molten need, knowing exactly where and how to press, how hard or soft to rub, how fast or slow to go. She keened, lurched with sensations almost too much to bear. And that was before he dipped two fingers inside her. It again made her feel so acutely how empty she felt. How only having him inside her had ever filled the void.

"Take me, Raiden. No foreplay...please."

In answer, with movements that bordered on magic in their efficiency, he rid her of her every garment, had her naked beneath him in under ten seconds. Before she could fumble with his zipper to release him, clutch him to her and bring him inside her, he slid down her body.

Protesting weakly, yet unable to do anything

but surrender, she arched helplessly as he triggered her every erogenous inch, which under his hands was every last one she had. Again and again she tried to drag him up to her until his magnificent head settled between her thighs and his lips and tongue scorched the heart of her femininity. The sight and the concept of what he did to her were even more incapacitating than the physical sensations.

Through the delirium, she watched him cosset her, drink her, revel in her essence, in her need and taste and pleasure. Then, as always, he knew exactly when she could take no more.

His lips suckled her nub, his teeth grazing it even as his fingers strummed her inner trigger. But it was his command that snapped the coil of unbearable tension inside her.

"Let me see and hear how much I pleasure you, Scarlett."

Shrieking with the recoil of sensation, her body heaved in a chain reaction. She held his eyes all through, as he always demanded that she did in the throes, letting him see what he was doing to her.

Finally subsiding, unable even to regulate her

breathing, she watched through drugged eyes as he began again, varying his method, renewing her desperation, deepening her surrender.

She knew there was no point in begging for him again. He'd do with her as he pleased. And give her pleasure beyond endurance while at it.

It would be wise to save her breath for the screams of soul-racking ecstasy he would inflict on her all night long.

And if a voice in her drugged mind told her this would end with a far worse scar than in the past, she didn't care.

The end was still weeks away. And she was savoring what she could have with him until the very last second....

The first thing Raiden saw as soon as he opened his eyes was Scarlett. He had to blink to make sure he actually saw her. Nowadays he saw her whether she was there or not. She was all that filled his mind's eye, his every thought and fantasy.

But she was really here this time. Barely. She'd already showered, dressed and packed her famous overnight bag. Her bag of tricks, as she'd once teasingly referred to it. She did have it filled with stuff that tricked his senses into catapulting to a higher realm. Lingerie, oils and an array of surprising enhancers of her own concoction.

Not that those things were what affected him. They did only because it was she who wore them, who wielded them. Now the bag was over her shoulder and she was about to walk out of his bedroom.

Since they'd started their arrangement six weeks ago, this was the first time he'd woken up before she'd left. Which was unbelievable. Not that he'd woken up this time, but that he'd actually slept through all the other times. As someone whose senses had been conditioned to be on full alert all the time, he'd never relaxed around anyone so fully, not even his brothers, to let sleep claim him so completely.

But against all the reasons he had to distrust her, Raiden's instincts told him otherwise. They trusted her implicitly, turned off his every built-in alarm system, to the point that they made him sleep—deep, blissful, rejuvenating sleep—only while beside her. And to continue surrendering to slumber even as she puttered around his domain, knowing he was his safest with her around.

But it never failed. She always left first thing in the morning, never once waking him up to say goodbye. He'd hoped today would be different, since he'd told her he wouldn't go to work before noon today. He'd hoped she'd take this as what he'd meant it to be, an invitation to sleep in with him and have a late breakfast together.

But then why should he feel so disappointed that she hadn't heeded his implication? Beyond the relentless demands he made on her sexually, in anything else he maintained a take-it-or-leave-it attitude. She probably didn't even realize there'd been an invitation hidden in his words.

But his attitude was just a front. In reality, every second he spent in her company, the bad memories of the past faded, as if they'd happened to someone else. He could no longer see her through their tainted prism. He believed he now saw through to her core self, the real woman. He believed he felt what she felt. Though she was vocal only in passion, he could swear he sensed that this was no longer purely sexual to her. If it had ever been.

And he wasn't deluding himself about this. He'd been feeling this even before learning the truth about her current work made him radically change his opinion of her character.

When he'd first investigated her activities in Japan, he'd thought her humanitarian work with UNICEF was just an ingenious way of wheedling herself into major businessmen's pockets, like Hiro, for donations she'd pocket herself. Then she'd asked for the hundred million, stating it would all be used in her work. He hadn't been in a condition at the time to care why she'd asked for it, had vaguely thought she'd had to at least be exaggerating about the money's intended use. But after he'd given her the money, and she continued working harder than ever, he had to revise his suspicions, since he'd given her more than ten years' worth of donation drives could raise.

Further investigations had revealed the incredible results she'd been consistently getting for the past three years, fifteen months of those in Japan. Everything fell into place in the light of his new time with her. And that was before he'd discovered her most ambitious project was being funded by her own money. The money she'd taken from him.

He'd then realized she'd asked him for it only so it would free her from dependence on donations and other sources of official funding. Those had been limiting the scope of what she could achieve, and she was always threatened by being forced to stop her projects altogether if she ran out of money. He'd even traced parts of the previous sum he'd given her to more of her humanitarian efforts. He now had no doubt the rest of it had been put to very good use, as she'd told him that first night. He'd thought she was being provocative, but she'd only been telling him the truth. And expecting him to believe the worst.

But even doing so, with the way he'd been feeling, he would have given her a billion dollars had she asked. The way he was feeling now, if she asked, he'd sign over all his assets.

Now he watched her from slit eyes as she paused at the door of his expansive bedroom and looked back. In her utilitarian clothes and ponytail, she looked so practical, so young. So fragile. She'd lost a lot of weight in the past six weeks, and he could sometimes swear she was reverting to what she'd been before.

She hadn't realized he'd woken up. And the expression that came over her, the emotions that gripped her features when she thought she was safe from his scrutiny, speared through him.

Such wistfulness, such pervasive dejection.

Long after she'd closed the door and he heard her leave his penthouse, he lay there on his back in the bed in which they'd shared indescribable intimacies, staring at the ceiling.

Why was she feeling that way? *Did* she feel that way?

He couldn't tell for sure. Not as long as he didn't know everything there was to know about her.

What he knew now was just feelings, observations and information about her current status. Her past remained as inaccessible as ever.

After that night three weeks ago, when she'd told him why she'd chosen the name Scarlett, her red hair and that specific face, she'd gone back to evading his probing. Beyond being candid about what she thought in the moment, and explicit about what he made her feel physically, she gave him nothing more that could make it possible to reconstruct her past.

A past he could no longer bear not knowing about.

It was no longer to tie up everything about her neatly, so that when their time together came to an end, he'd stow away her memory in a closed file and move on, with no lingering uncertainties keeping her alive in his memory. Not that he'd ever wanted *that.* He now admitted it to himself that when he'd hit the first dead ends in his search into her past, he'd convinced himself she was untraceable. He'd unconsciously wanted to avoid finding out what would disturb him more. Or worse, what would irrevocably eradicate her from his mind.

Now it was different. This woman he'd been sharing every intimacy he'd never wanted to share with another with *was* the woman he'd thought she was in the past. She'd told the truth when she'd said she'd never acted with him. And she'd never made personal use of the money she'd taken from him, except to build a new persona. He had to find out what had driven her to that mercenary life in the past, then to go through such effort and pain to escape it.

Yet he didn't know how to start a new investigation, or if one would actually lead to anything other than more dead ends.

But he *could* investigate someone close to her. Hiro. His past was heavily documented, and maybe some threads from her relationship with him would lead to unraveling her mystery.

Investigating Scarlett's relationship with Hiro turned out to be a simple matter of entering their names in an internet search engine.

At the click of a button, he got dozens of results detailing the incident that had brought them together.

About a year ago, Hiro was on one of his private jets, returning from a charity event on Kyoto. Scarlett was among the dozen people who'd organized the event and had been invited to go back to Tokyo with him. Then the plane was hit by lightning.

Five people died in the crash, and others had assorted injuries but had managed to pull themselves out of the wreckage. But Hiro was trapped.

They'd tried to extricate him, but on realizing the plane was about to explode, they'd run out, leaving him to his fate. All but Scarlett.

Risking her own life, she'd refused to leave him even when he'd begged her to save herself. She'd finally managed to drag him free and away from the plane in the nick of time. Then she'd stopped the bleeding from the major artery in his leg, which would have killed him anyway, and continued to care for him until rescue teams arrived. Through it all, she'd ignored her own injuries.

Hiro had been on record so many times in the media lauding Scarlett's fearlessness and heroism, and stating unequivocally that he owed her his life.

In addition to the press coverage Raiden found, his own investigations revealed they'd been best friends ever since, but that there'd been no hint of romantic involvement in their closeness. Apart from their friendship, Hiro had been donating massive amounts of money to her causes. But there was never enough money to establish the ongoing services she was setting up. And it was far better to have personal money she had immediate access to, since Hiro's donations would always be tied in lengthy legal procedures before being made available for her to use.

That further proved Scarlett was the person he'd always felt her to be, and that what she'd told him about her and Hiro was true. That revelation cleared away his last misconception about her.

But it still gave him no insight into her past.

Which meant there was one last option open to him.

Enlisting the combined investigative powers of his brothers.

He'd never before considered doing that. It had been the last thing he'd wanted—for them to find out about her, and about how close he'd come to unwittingly exposing them all.

But discovering the truth about her had become imperative. It now meant more to him than learning the truth about himself ever did.

Six

"So there's a woman out there who knows everything about you. And you deem to tell us now? Five years after the fact?"

Raiden looked steadily across his executive desk at the three juggernauts who sat facing him in a semicircle, looking like a tribunal of demigods.

They were the three of his six brothers who'd been able to come for the face-to-face meeting. He'd just told them the short version of his history with Hannah/Scarlett.

The first one to talk after he'd finished was Numair, the leader of the Black Castle brotherhood. His leader.

Numair Al Aswad, or Phantom, the name he'd known him by for their twenty years in The Organization's prison, had been the oldest among them and the one who'd been there longest. Each had found him already established as The Organization's rising star when they'd come to the prison they'd eventually called Black Castle. Almost twenty-five of Numair's forty years had been spent there, at first being trained, then later training others, starting with them. He had taught them his every stealthy and lethal method in espionage and execution.

He hadn't only been the best operative in The Organization's history, he'd also been the shrewdest, the one who'd chosen Raiden and his brothers out of hundreds of boys, judging them to be not only the best of the best but kindred spirits. Taking them on, making them his team, he'd guided them through the endless years of captivity. He was the one who'd forged their brotherhood and their blood oath to one day escape, amass wealth and power and bring down those who'd sold them as slaves and The Organization itself.

Numair had worked to that end since he'd been only ten. It had been his mind-bogglingly convoluted and long-term plan that had made it possible for them to finally escape, disappear and create their new identities. He and Richard, Rafael's former handler, had also been the ones who'd led them into creating Black Castle Enterprises.

But like Raiden, Numair had remembered no specific details about his family before he'd been sold to The Organization. He'd only remembered a few names. One he'd ended up calling himself. The others he'd long realized were those of desert kingdoms. He'd searched, like Raiden, for his bloodline since their escape, and he'd recently found out that not only did he come from one of those kingdoms, but before his abduction, he'd been the heir to its throne.

But reclaiming his legacy wouldn't be as easy as it was for Raiden. Numair's return to his kingdom would turn his region upside down. It could even ignite a war.

Which was fine by Numair. Nothing would stop him from claiming what was his. And it wouldn't be the first time he'd instigated armed conflicts.

Now he regarded Raiden with eyes as still and fathomless as an abyss. But his absolute calmness didn't fool him. That abyss was filled with flesh-melting acid.

Raiden had compromised everything Numair had strived for—their freedoms, their achievements, their very lives. Numair was coldly angry. And when he was like this, he was deadly. Anyone with any sense of self-preservation would be afraid. Very afraid.

"So what took you so long to let us know?" That was Wildcard. Of Russian origins, he'd come to The Organization old enough to remember his past life. But he'd chosen not to make contact with his family after his escape, adopting the name Ivan Kostantinov instead. Still a Russian name, but he hadn't told any of them the significance of his choice. Many of his rivals in the cyber development world thought Ivan the Terrible suited him far more.

Ivan's mockery grew more caustic when Raiden made no response. "Did you change your name from Lightning to Turtle without telling us?"

"Maybe since he's a ninja, he's always been one."

Ivan glared at Bones, the most blasé of the brothers. If only in comparison to the rest of them. To the rest of the world Antonio Balducci was a whirlwind of energy and achievements, an enigmatic, awe-inspiring figure who was a wizard in medicine and with the women who catapulted themselves at his feet. As their former medical expert and field surgeon, Antonio was now in charge of Black Castle's medical R&D business and a reconstructive-trauma surgical god whose work bordered on magic.

On the personal level, ever since their days in Black Castle, Antonio and Ivan couldn't stop harassing each other, but neither one could live without the other, either.

"You knew that she knew," Ivan said, resuming the corrosive scolding Antonio had interrupted. "And you not only let her go then, you're back with her again now. Don't you—"

"I had no idea what she was up to until it was too late," Raiden interrupted Ivan. "I let her go because she gave me her word she'd never use her knowledge. She kept it and I—"

"You had no way of knowing she would," Numair interrupted him in turn. "That was a blind, insane gamble. You jeopardized yourself and, by association, all of us. You compounded your mistakes when you made the decision to keep us in the dark. It could have meant our very lives."

From the bare facts, it did look like that, Raiden conceded. But it had been his gut feeling that he'd gone with then. Still, he couldn't admit that. It would make him look even more unreliable, and Scarlett more dangerous.

He finally exhaled. "I made the call to believe her. And I was right to."

Antonio snorted. "How do you know that? There's no proof yet that this woman hasn't leaked strategic info about you, or us, in the past five years. For all we know, every single problem or loss we suffered could have been her doing."

Raiden's answering snort was more spectacular. "Don't you think if she'd leaked info about our identities, the least we would have suffered would have been bullets between the eyes, not the tame business setbacks we did? She leaked, and will leak, nothing."

Antonio shrugged. "Then you lucked out. So far."

"It wasn't luck. It was a judgment. I stand by it."

"I can understand you making a mistake once," Ivan said. "Though I can't get my head around it, not from you. But to be doing it again… That's totally incomprehensible to me."

"Whatever mistake I made in the past, none of the same variables apply now. I'm not making a mistake again."

Ivan's lips twisted condescendingly. "Says the man whose wedding is in three weeks. The wedding that will secure your entry into the family you've searched for for ten years, an ultraconservative clan who would reject you at the slightest whiff of scandal."

Antonio shook his head. "And you didn't even wait until all the legalities were concluded and you had your family name back to indulge your desire for this black widow."

Ivan nodded. "You are risking everything you've dreamed of and planned for all your life by associating with this woman at this critical time. And worst of all, it seems you don't realize you're doing that."

Oh, he did realize. Especially in the past week, since he'd dropped his precautions, had been surprising Scarlett at work, insisting on taking her out, then to and from home, no longer able to bear getting there or leaving separately, or any other secrecy measures.

When she'd at first refused to relinquish their precautions, he'd insisted he knew what he was doing. Which he certainly didn't. The only thing he knew was that he could no longer compartmentalize her presence in his life. He wanted her with him in every possible moment, couldn't bear wasting the time he could have with her on secrecy procedures. How that would ultimately affect his plans, he was at a stage where he no longer cared. He knew his time with her was draining away like accelerated sand in an hourglass, and such a realization was messing with his restraint, rearranging all of his priorities.

From his brothers' point of view, that would all prove that he'd lost his mind. He couldn't contest their diagnosis. For he had no sanity to speak of when it came to Scarlett.

When he didn't make a comment, Antonio exhaled. "From her own admission, she's a Mata Hari who's played at least five dozen men before you. You think you're so special to her that she won't do the same to you...again? How could you resume your liaison after she blackmailed you for fifty million dollars?"

"I did after she asked for double that this time." The trio of his brothers just stared at him as if he'd sprouted two extra heads. "Apart from the money she used to create her current identity, she only uses the money in her humanitarian work."

"And you realized that when?" Ivan scoffed. "Long after the fact, I'm certain. This woman demands money, and no matter how outrageous the amount, and whether you have reason to succumb to her demands or not, you give it to her. Without consulting any of us."

"And without letting us know of the danger she could have posed to all of us back then, and could still pose now or any time in the future."

Antonio shook his head in incredulity. "This is even worse than I at first thought."

Raiden's gaze swept the three men, felt them passing judgment. From the fury on Ivan's face, the dismay on Antonio's and the nothingness on Numair's, he knew the sentence they would like to pass was a painless death. To put him out of their collective misery.

Cocking his head at them, he sighed. "Are you done?"

"Actually, no," Ivan growled. "How did you expect us to take this? Don't you realize the magnitude of what you risked? And are still risking?"

Numair sat forward, moving in pure effortlessness, the first trait that had earned him the name Phantom before the rest of his stealthy methods had. This meant he'd decided this back-and-forth exchange was over. He'd reached his verdict.

"Give me one reason why I shouldn't leave this office and go eliminate this woman's threat."

Silence detonated in the wake of Numair's tranquil words.

Feeling his heart about to do the same, Raiden drew in a sharp breath. Once Numair made up his mind, nothing could stop him. So Raiden had to stop his mind in its tracks before it latched on to a course of action.

"One reason. Me." His voice was a steel blade as he transferred his gaze from Numair to the others, letting them know Scarlett was one line he'd never let anyone cross. Not even them. Then he let the lifetime of history and empathy between them enter his gaze. "We survived hell, then conquered the world by trusting each other absolutely. You depended on me and my instincts countless times. I now ask you to trust the instincts that never led us wrong."

"They led you wrong in her case," Antonio pointed out.

"No, they haven't. I now believe she'd been forced to spy on me. And this is why I called this meeting, why I told you about her. I need you to help me find out exactly who she is, and how Medvedev found her, and what power he had over her."

"She was a professional honey trap with a long history behind her before Medvedev hired her," Antonio dismissed.

"And I want to find out how that happened, how she'd entered this life, the life she'd gone to such lengths to exit." He gave them a moment to absorb his demands and the new considerations, then went on. "Promise me you'll do everything in your power to help me settle this issue once and for all."

"I can certainly settle her issue with no effort at all." Numair's voice was laced with chilling, hair-raising humor.

"Numair."

At Raiden's booming growl, Numair held his enraged gaze for seconds before he shrugged. "It would be better for you and for all of us if she just…disappeared. If this were my call, I wouldn't forgive anyone who betrayed me. Not for any reason. If I were you, I wouldn't care why she did."

"You're not me, Numair. Now give me your word."

Numair inclined his head vaguely, looking like a malevolent genie from an Oriental fable with his shoulder-length black hair, slanting eyebrows and striking features.

"Give me your *oath,* Phantom," Raiden gritted.

He had to have that, or Numair would leave his office and fulfill his not-so-veiled threat. When it came to protecting their brotherhood, Numair would do, and had done, literally anything. But he also had an unswerving code of honor, would give his life to uphold an oath he'd made. But he had to make it first, unequivocally, not just imply it, before it became binding.

Pursing his lips, Numair regarded him with the same steadiness he had since Raiden had first seen him when he'd been five, that of the stern older brother who knew best. He didn't approve, but he now realized that Raiden wasn't defending his mistakes in the past or his whims now. He was defending the woman he wanted with every fiber of his being.

Though he still had no reason to make that oath, none but Raiden's conviction, Numair finally said, "You have it."

"I don't have good news."

Raiden's heart rammed his ribs viciously at Numair's declaration.

Numair hadn't stood up to receive him when Abbas, his right-hand man, had let Raiden into his presidential suite at the Mandarin Oriental Hotel. He said nothing more than his opening statement. Instead, he continued staring out of the window at the glittering nighttime Tokyo as Raiden approached him.

Raiden barely noticed his luxurious surroundings as he came to stand before him. Numair only leaned forward on the immaculate brown silk sofa and poured himself a straight whiskey from a crystal decanter. Still without looking at Raiden, he tossed the shot back.

It hadn't surprised Raiden when only four days after his meeting with his trio of brothers, it had been Numair who'd called him to tell him he had what Raiden had been looking for.

As Phantom, his investigative capabilities were unmatched. Now as Numair Al Aswad, or Black Panther as he was known in the intelligence field, where he was now one of the world's biggest experts and contractors, his reach had multiplied a hundredfold. The only one who could rival him was Richard, or Cobra, Rafael's past handler. Not that he'd even considered enlisting Richard's help. Not because he still felt any hard feelings toward him as one of their past captors, but because of the way Numair felt about him.

There *was* still a possibility those two might end up killing each other. Whatever made the two forces of nature abhor each other so much, even after becoming allies, neither man would ever say.

Dread eating through the rest of his tattered control, he gritted his teeth. "Just give me what you have."

Numair at last looked up at him. His eyes weren't indifferent anymore. They were heavy.

Then he said, "Sit down. And pour yourself a drink."

He complied, because his legs no longer felt able to support him. He descended heavily onto the armchair across from Numair, a fine tremor traversing his grip as he poured himself a shot. "It's that bad?"

"Worse."

The fist squeezing Raiden's heart tightened as Numair reached for a tablet on the coffee table between them, accessed an app, then pushed the tablet toward Raiden. Raiden stopped its slide, and his heart turned over in his chest at what he saw on the screen.

A photo of an exquisite girl with shimmering

dark caramel hair, an impassive face and extinguished eyes. A younger version of the Hannah he'd known, with a different hair color. And without the warm, lighthearted, normal expressions. This was her without the act. The real her. A girl without hope.

His upper lip and forehead beading with sweat, he glanced up at Numair, his insides churning.

Numair answered his unspoken question. "That's Katya Petrovna, whom you knew as Hannah McPherson and now know as Scarlett Delacroix."

Katya. Her real name at last. It suited her. As anything did. She made anything hers. Names, hair color, faces. Him.

Numair went on. "She was born in Tbilisi, Georgia, in the former U.S.S.R., and raised on the Black Sea coast of the Russian Riviera. She was a descendant of a Georgian noble house. Then, during the collapse of the Soviet Union, she was seven when she was separated from her mother in a riot. She ended up in a white slavery ring."

The thudding of his heart escalated until it shook his whole body. There could be a hundred possibilities after this point, all ugly and horrific. But he had the terrible feeling he knew exactly where this was going.

Then Numair validated his suspicions. "By the age of ten, she ended up in The Organization's grasp."

Even though he'd already suspected that, all his nerves loosened with the blow of confirmation.

The crystal glass in his hand crashed on the marble floor in a thousand diamond-like splinters.

Scarlett. Or Hannah. Or Katya. *Her.* She'd been The Organization's slave, too. Just like him. Like all of them.

Without batting an eye at the smashed glass, Numair tossed back another shot as if he needed it. Then he continued. "She was one of hundreds of girls who'd been imprisoned in an all-female installation equivalent to our Black Castle. And like us, the girls were categorized according to their abilities and talents, but also according to their looks. All girls were trained as we were, but the beautiful ones had extra training in seduction and manipulation. They were used as sexual bait for the world's movers and shakers, or anyone The Organization wanted breached, entrapped or untraceably terminated. According to my source, she was the best. But her trail ended five years ago, when she clearly faked her death."

Raiden struggled not to howl in agony. The details Numair had just related so clinically painted a gruesome picture of the life of the girl in the photo. A girl who knew she was lost and no one would ever come to her rescue. Who knew she'd be a hostage forever, living a life of danger and degradation, an instrument in the service of whoever paid her masters for her skills, to be used and abused as they willed. A woman who knew that escape was impossible, and the only way out was death.

He'd started this quest for the truth, hoping to find out she'd been forced to betray him. Now he wished she hadn't been. Being right meant she'd suffered unimaginably, must be scarred for life. Now he would have given anything for her to be just a woman who'd entered the wrong path, then decided to change, to make good.

But she wasn't. She'd been enslaved. And he couldn't bear thinking she'd suffered what he had. And far, far worse.

"I now believe you were right," Numair said.

"She won't expose you or any of us. Not when it means ultimately exposing herself, too. We're all in the same boat, so to speak."

He wanted to roar to Numair that he was still wrong, that this wasn't why his and their secrets were safe with Scarlett. But his vocal cords felt fused over molten agony.

"Bottom line is, you can go ahead and indulge your desire for her. As long as you don't jeopardize your relevant plans." Numair stopped, as if debating whether to tell him more or not. Then he exhaled. "There something else you need to know."

In minutes, Numair stopped talking, and suddenly Raiden could no longer bear hearing another word.

He heaved up to his feet before the roaring inside him escaped his lips.

At the suite's door, Numair's warning hit him between the shoulder blades.

"Don't tell her anything."

"Why didn't you tell me?"

Scarlett had known something was wrong the moment she'd entered the penthouse to find

Raiden facing the door as if he'd been waiting for her for hours. His hands and face were clenched as he asked that question.

In a heartbeat, she knew what this blazing darkness cloaking him was all about.

He knew the truth. Her truth.

She didn't have to ask how, didn't need to. He just did.

She felt exposed, her every sordid secret on display before the one person with whom she'd wanted to retain a measure of mystery and allure. She knew there was no point in prevaricating.

So she shrugged. "What was the point?"

"What…?" He seemed so stunned by her answer he found nothing to say. Then he blurted out, "You don't consider being the victim of the same organization that'd kidnapped and enslaved me relevant?"

"Not really." She sat down before she collapsed. "Not now that we both got out."

Urgent strides brought him standing above her, and then he descended on the couch beside her, taking both her hands in his. "I need you to tell me everything. I know only who you were, how you ended up in The Organization's hands, how they trained and used you, like they did me. Now I need to know the specifics of your mission targeting me."

She'd always wished she could erase those specifics from her memory and psyche as she'd erased her former identity. Or thought she had. She hadn't. Raiden had found everything out.

But to avoid telling him the full truth would only prolong the torture. She should get it over with. What they had would soon be over. His wedding was in sixteen days.

She left her hands in his, not because his touch and urgency didn't burn her, but because she couldn't pull away.

Barely holding herself together, she started to explain.

"Medvedev worked on occasion on our side of the operation. He was my handler's lover. She was the one who recommended me to him when he described the skillset he required to set you up. I realized later this was his personal vengeance on you, and if he was right, he wanted it to be his triumph, and his secret shame if he was wrong. He told my handler no specifics.

Though he must have told her something lucrative enough to get her to make The Organization believe I was on a mission for them. She gave me all the time I needed to take care of you. Medvedev told her not to worry about watching me, since he'd do it, and he would deliver me back to her at the completion of my task."

She paused to adjust her breathing, which had started to hitch under his laserlike eyes.

"It was a very difficult task, he told me, since your records were somehow expunged from The Organization's system. There were no photos, no fingerprints, no voice recognition, no retinal scans and no DNA to match. Even your implanted tracking devices were deactivated. I assume that was your doing." Raiden nodded, then gestured his impatience. She continued, almost choking on every word. "His only evidence was that you resembled his escapee, and he had a feeling about you. But he couldn't build a case on mere resemblance and his feelings. He needed evidence. Evidence I had to provide."

Pretending to adjust her position, she pulled away from him. He only compensated, touching her along her whole left side, zapping every inch of her flesh with agitation. She had to spit out a conclusion and hope it would satisfy him.

"When I asked what would happen if I couldn't get close enough to you or if it took too long to do so, he said not to worry. He'd do everything to give me all the resources and time I needed to get him his proof. Then, I guess to make me committed to his cause, he said if I got him the proof he needed, he would ensure my freedom from The Organization."

Everything she'd said so far had been specifics of the facts he had already known or deduced. Nothing seemed to surprise him.

She went on, "He said he'd extort you for a huge sum, pretending it was his price for not exposing you. He said he'd give me a portion of the money to build a new life for myself, and to fake my death so The Organization wouldn't look for me. Just promising me that behind my handler's back, he told me he would betray anyone to get what he wanted, starting with me. But I had no option but to do as he wanted, and to keep his secret. It was clearly implied my life depended on both actions." She paused, taking a shallow, shaky breath. "The rest you know. I came after you with my fabricated identity, and we became lovers until I slipped and you found me out. We made the deal and I managed to escape Medvedev after misleading him. I used the money to create a new identity and fake the death of the old one."

She fell silent, but Raiden's eyes continued to set her every nerve aflame. He was waiting for her to confess more.

She couldn't. The rest was just too horrible.

When he made sure she wasn't adding more, Raiden faced her fully. "Knowing Medvedev and his obsession with me, and what I cost him when I escaped him, being thwarted once wouldn't have stopped him. He would have never stopped. That was the biggest question I had when you told me he was the one who recruited you—how he let you go, how he didn't come after me again. But now I know how."

Her heart stopped as she prayed he only thought he did.

Then he went on and her prayers were aborted.

"He died five years ago, stabbed in the eye

in a hotel room." His eyes turned to infernos as he pulled her closer. "It was you who killed him, wasn't it?"

Seven

Raiden's words weren't a question. Just a statement demanding only the corroboration of details. They ricocheted in Scarlett's head until she felt it would burst.

It was you who killed him, wasn't it?

Needing to silence the reverberations, she tore herself out of his hold, feeling as if her flesh had peeled in his hands.

But he wouldn't let her get far. He caught her back into a fierce embrace. "Just tell me, Scarlett."

The terrible memories welled like poison-tinged ink in her system. "Please, Raiden. Don't make me."

His embrace tightened, the hand pressing her head into his expansive chest, convulsing as if he wanted to push her into his rib cage, hide her inside him. "Let it all out, Scarlett. Let me relieve you of it. Let me take it all on for you."

She writhed in his hold, as if she was drowning and trying to kick to the surface. But he held her tighter, letting her know he wasn't letting it go this time. For he must know she hadn't told him everything. Not only about Medvedev but about her, them, everything. And he wouldn't be satisfied with anything less than the whole truth now.

Unable to make such confessions while in his arms, she choked, "I'll tell you everything… just…just let me breathe."

Cursing himself ferociously, Raiden let her go at once, thinking he'd been suffocating her. She didn't have enough breath to tell him he wasn't the one starving her of oxygen. It was the thought of letting go.

It was harder than she'd expected to let go of the masks she'd hidden behind since she was seven years old. Tearing off her facade was almost as scary as the thought of tearing a layer of skin off her face.

She sat there beside him, feeling his empathic gaze sear her, gathering every spark of will and courage to do what she must do. Show him the real her for the first time.

Inhaling one last bracing breath, she looked him in the eyes and let her barriers crumble.

Raiden's eyes shot wider, his nostrils flared, his chest deflating as if she'd punched him in the gut. That meant she'd managed to show him inside her. And it flabbergasted him.

She let go of her last reluctance. "About Medvedev…"

A finger on her lips stopped her halting words, his face gripped with emotions she'd never seen. They were so complex, she couldn't fathom them. "Start at the beginning, Scarlett. Tell me everything from before you approached me."

Nothing but every last detail would satisfy him, would it? As it shouldn't. She owed him at least that.

Nodding, she let out a ragged exhalation. "Before I did, I investigated you, as I always did, to tailor my approach to every…case. But you were an enigma, with no information indicating your character. So I watched you, and from my observations, I knew you wouldn't respond favorably to a direct approach, wouldn't respond to overt seduction, like almost all men in my experience."

His teeth gritted, his frown deepening. No doubt he hated hearing how he'd been a mission, how there'd been so many before him.

But she already knew he'd feel that way, and she was only telling him the details of what he already knew. So she continued.

"I set up that car accident, created that steeped-in-normalcy persona, because I'd judged only a woman like the fictional Hannah McPherson would have the best chance to make you feel safe enough to let her come close. And I was right."

His hand grabbed the back of her head, his eyes so fierce, as if trying to compel her to believe him. "You were wrong. It was you, the woman beneath the act that I responded to. I proved that when I responded to you again, when you projected a totally different persona." His hand gentled at her nape, making her melt in his grip. "But you said you never acted with me.

Was that because once you met me, you judged I would respond best to the real you?"

And she made the first irrevocable confession. "Until I met you, I didn't know there was a real me."

His eyes flared like supernovas, and his grip twisted in her hair with the same ferocity, making her gasp with pleasure and ratcheting heartache.

Suddenly, confessions felt like poison she had to spit out. "From the moment I met you, all my scenarios evaporated, and I was unable to be anything with you but the person you knew, the person I didn't realize existed. It was with you that I became aware of my true personality." At his groan, she turned her face into his shoulder, escaping the intensity in his eyes. "I realized almost at once that I was actually feeling something for you. And among all the dangers I ever faced, those unknown feelings were the most dangerous thing that ever happened to me. It was as though you were my first intimacy. And you were. Any other man I've been with was a mission, an evil I've been forced to endure with a seductive smile while my soul retched or, at best, was numb."

"Scarlett…"

She burrowed into his chest, unable to let him interrupt. The floodgates had opened and everything came gushing out. "It was with you that my senses were awakened for the first time and I realized what intimacy was, what transfiguring passion felt like. You were my first pleasure… then you become my first and, I'm certain, my last love."

Never. Never in his wildest dreams had Raiden expected this. His best hope had been that she'd tell him the truth, and that it would include an admission to validate his feelings. That he hadn't been just a mission to her, that she'd felt something real for him. Then, and now. Never had he dared wish she'd say anything near the things she'd just said.

But she'd said them. She felt them. Had always felt them.

And it felt as if the last barrier he'd erected inside him to protect himself from the heartache she'd caused came crashing down. Admissions rushed in, swamping him in the truth of his emotions for her.

Just as she'd come to life with him, so had he with her. Just as he was her first and last intimacy, her one and only love, so was she his.

Emotions rose like a tidal wave inside him.

With trembling hands he tried to lift her head from where she'd buried it into his chest, needing communion with her in those transfiguring moments. "Scarlett, darling, please, let me…"

Resisting him, she kept her head plastered over his thundering heart, words rushing out of her again, drowning whatever he would have said. "But it wasn't only when I realized I'd fallen in love with you that it became imperative I ended the danger to you. From the first moment I met you, I knew you weren't one of the sleazebags or criminals I was always sent after, and who deserved everything I did to them and more. You were everything I didn't think existed—a noble man who used your powers for the greater good, and who never advertised your benevolence. It was by following in your steps that I ended up in my line of work now."

She raised her head then, and he felt as if he

got a direct blow to the heart. Her eyes. God, her eyes.

The emotions in them were staggering. As if everything she'd ever suppressed, ever hidden from him, from the whole world, was flooding out. He felt submerged.

She threaded shaking hands in his hair, such tenderness in her touch and gaze. "Then I found out that you were like me, but that you had escaped when I knew I never would. If I loved you with all my newly forged heart before that, I loved you even more then, with the broken parts of me before the whole ones I discovered inside me because of you. All I cared about from then on was protecting you at all costs."

Her hands smoothed over his head, chest and shoulders, becoming feverish, as if she wanted to make sure he was here, safe, whole, and that she had protected him.

"To protect you, I had to throw Medvedev off your scent. So I stalled him until I figured out how to prove you weren't his escaped agent, and to be with you for as long as I could."

Every word she said felt like a stab, their collective pain pouring out of him on a butchered groan. "Why didn't you tell me everything? I would have taken care of Medvedev and saved you from The Organization."

Her eyes shot up to his, the tears filling them rippling like a pool in an earthquake. It was clear she'd never thought this even an option.

"Did you fear I'd punish you if I knew the truth?"

Her expression made it clear that wasn't something she'd considered, either. "I was only afraid you'd go after Medvedev, and I couldn't risk you. He was an unpredictable monster."

He grimaced at her misplaced fear. "Didn't you know enough about me to know I could have handled Medvedev in my sleep? Or did you think I would, but still wouldn't help you?"

Her eyes implored his belief, when he'd sooner doubt himself rather than her now. "I only cared about your safety and the new life you'd built. And I wanted to end Medvedev's danger to you without you finding out the truth about me and how I came to be with you. I wanted to remain the one you trusted implicitly, wanted totally. I couldn't bear seeing the trust and passion in your eyes turn to contempt and disgust if you knew. I wanted to hold on to the memories. Those months with you, the way you looked at me, the way you treated me, meant more to me than anything."

"More than your life?"

"Yes."

He stared at her, the implications of her cried out affirmation boggling his mind.

She'd truly thought holding on to her memories and to his good opinion of her more important than escaping her enslavement, or even preserving her life.

Being unable to reach into the past to make her realize that he would have forgiven her anything, that there'd been nothing to forgive, corroded his sanity. Her false belief had deprived him of the chance to protect her, save her.

He couldn't even avenge her. Medvedev was already dead.

But, no. He'd been working to bring down The Organization—for himself, his brothers and all the unknown children who had been abused. But now, more than ever, he would destroy it on her behalf. His vengeance would now know no bounds. He would wreak unimaginable pain on everyone who'd had a hand in a single moment of her suffering. And when she hadn't told him the worst parts yet... Though he no longer knew if he could withstand hearing them.

But he would, no matter what it did to him. He had to relieve her of all of her burdens, in every way he could.

A distant look came into her eyes. "But all my precautions were in vain. When you called me that last time, the moment I heard your voice I knew you'd found me out. I knew it was the end and I wasn't ready. I would have never been ready. Everything I feared came to pass. You sounded as I always dreaded—angry and disillusioned and disgusted. I was only grateful I didn't see all that on your face. And there was only one thing I could do. Make it all worse."

She looked into his eyes with everything she was on display for the first time. And it was beyond his imagining.

"I wanted to disappear," she said. "Make it impossible for Medvedev to find me. I also wanted to help others in my same situation, but I knew our collective freedoms would cost a huge amount of money. So I blackmailed you for it. That also served to end everything between us on the worst note possible.

"But before I could leave the country, Medvedev walked into the hotel room where I was under a false name. He was shrewd enough to sense I'd make a run for it. I told him I just wanted to escape The Organization, that I thought he wouldn't come through for me since I only had proof you weren't his agent. But he was convinced I had proof you were, even deducted I'd blackmailed you myself, though he assigned me purely mercenary motives for that. He said once I gave him the info, he wouldn't only extort you himself, but your partners, too, whom he was certain were the other operatives who escaped, making this more lucrative than he'd ever thought."

She paused to draw in a shuddering breath. "I failed to divert him, and he just knew everything. I knew he'd turn your hard-won freedom into a new prison, would end up turning you over to The Organization to redeem himself. The one card I had left was that he needed solid info, and I wouldn't give it to him. At first, he still promised he'd keep his end of the bargain if I did mine. But I refused, told him he couldn't do a thing without proof. And he started torturing me."

Something fundamental charred inside him. Red-hot wrath against a dead man he couldn't kill again almost ate through his arteries.

"I knew I wouldn't walk out of that room alive, but I could still save you if I took him down with me. With the last strength left in me, I stabbed him with a stiletto I used as a hair clip. I know how to kill a man with one strike, but he was no ordinary man. Instead of going into instant shock, he was all over me. He almost killed me…before he succumbed."

His whole body started shaking, on the verge of exploding. Scarlett had fought a monster like Medvedev and sustained near-fatal injuries… for him.

"I managed to stem my bleeding, to leave the hotel without being seen, to barely reach a secret medical center before I collapsed. It took them days to stabilize me."

She stopped, and her silence stretched. His blood burned and congealed in his arteries each single second.

Then she talked again, as if in a fugue. "As soon as I was well enough, I started acquiring this new face and a new identity. I came back here believing I'd have the painful pleasure of seeing you from afar without any danger of you recognizing me. But you did recognize me, and now you've even found out everything I thought would forever remain hidden."

Long minutes after she fell silent again, agonized beyond endurance, he choked out, "Why didn't you tell me all this when you met me again? When there was no more danger to me? Why did you let me think the worst of you?"

Suddenly her eyes looked exactly as they had in the photo Numair had showed him. Lifeless, hopeless. "Because there was no point. I came here thinking you'd long forgotten me. Then you recognized me and offered me this arrangement, and I knew I was just passing through your life. I only wanted to have this time with you before I moved on. I knew you'd go on to have the life you worked so hard to establish and you'd never think of me again. And I didn't want you to. I wanted to give you the closure I deprived you of the first time."

"I didn't want closure, Scarlett." He gripped her face, his hands shaking, needing her to know every single thing he'd felt all these years. "I lived all these years going insane for an explanation, *this* explanation. I was unable to come to terms with the discrepancy between what I felt with you, from you, and what it had seemed to be. I've been unable to have any kind of intimacy again."

"You mean you didn't...?" A tiny flame leaped in her eyes before it was immediately extinguished.

He crushed her in his arms, his heart convulsing at the despondence in her eyes. She'd never even considered it was possible for him to feel the same for her as she felt for him.

Needing to make her believe he'd always been hers, to erase every terrible moment she'd ever lived, he raised her face to his and held her eyes. "I didn't. I couldn't. I was yearning for the only woman I ever wanted, and it was excruciating because I thought you were a lie. But not only have you always been real and everything I ever craved and more, you protected me and my brothers from exposure. You saved our lives. And it almost cost you your own."

It cost me something more precious to me than my life.

Scarlett barely caught back the cry.

She couldn't let him know that. Not that. But she couldn't let him make it sound as if what she'd done had been a sacrifice. Giving him up had been that. Protecting him with her life had been a privilege.

She tried to wave his gratitude away, but he persisted.

"You must accept your dues. And you will have the gratitude and lifelong allegiance of my brothers, too. Yes, my partners in Black Castle Enterprises are all The Organization's escapees. We formed a brotherhood within our prison, swore a blood oath to escape, become unstoppable and bring down The Organization and anyone associated with it. We're going through the list from the outside in, and from bottom to top in such convoluted ways, they wouldn't know what hit them before they're destroyed." Suddenly he frowned, as if remembering something.

"What happened to the people you wanted to help?"

She remembered the friends who'd held her together all these years, before and after Raiden. They were now safe in their new lives, which made her aching lips spread in a smile of relief and thankfulness. "I got them out, built them new identities, too. I told you I put your money to the best use."

His gorgeous eyes poured what looked like pride over her, making her heart flutter like a hummingbird.

Then the frown of murderous wrath was back, even blacker. "Are the faint scars on your abdomen Medvedev's stabs?"

The noose of agonizing memories choked her again as she nodded, averting her gaze so she could tell the half-truth. "They were aesthetically revised during my other surgeries."

"Tell me he died in horrific pain."

At his vicious growl, she attempted a shrug. "Probably. I was too busy with my own pain and peril to notice his."

His fingers sank into her shoulders again.

"Why didn't you call me? For God's sake, Scarlett, did you think I wouldn't save you?"

His rage at the long-dead Medvedev was palpable. But it was his frustration with her, for not seeking his protection at first, then his help later that he seemed unable to handle. For a man like him, one who took charge and resolved problems, feeling helpless must be the worst thing that could happen to him. He must feel the same now, being unable to change the past.

"I told you what I thought," she murmured. "Contacting you again under any circumstances wasn't even an option."

"Even if you thought you were dying?"

"Especially then. I left to protect you. I would never have considered dragging you to a crime scene, risking your reputation and putting you under the law's scrutiny."

Her rationalizations seemed about to cause him an apoplectic fit. He seemed to vibrate as he struggled with bringing the tirades storming inside him under control.

Then he attacked on a different front, bombarding her with questions. "What were your injuries exactly? How long did it take you to heal? Do you suffer from any lasting damage or ongoing pain?"

I suffer both, she wanted to whimper.

But this was the one thing she wouldn't tell him. This was her loss and she couldn't let him share it.

But he would ask and push until he left her no place to hide any secrets. And she had to keep this one.

To shut him up, divert him, and because she couldn't bear wasting one more moment with him, she clung to him, her hands digging into his luxurious hair, tugging him closer. "No more questions, Raiden. I want you right this second."

He bared his teeth on a silent growl, his body lurching, tensing as if at the shock of a lash.

Peeling her hands off him with his own trembling ones, he held out a warning finger. "Don't, Scarlett. I'm not in control of myself. I was never in this condition."

Disregarding his warning, she lunged at him, tore his shirt out of his pants, attacked his zipper. "I want you out of control. I want you savage and rough and unable to stop. Take me hard and fast and now, Raiden. I can't wait. I *can't.*"

His harsh intakes of breath confessed his pleasure at her frenzy, but he ended it, capturing her feverish hands. When she writhed against him, raining bites and kisses anywhere she could reach, the last of his restraint crumbled, and she finally made him do what she wanted him to. He hauled her up in his arms and hurtled with her to his bed.

Once there, he flung her down onto her stomach, then launched himself over her, covering her with his great body. It was as if he was shielding her, hiding her, and poignancy welled out of her depths on a keen. Rumbling incessantly, he sounded like a beast, one protecting his mate, maddened and heartbroken he hadn't been able to prevent her injury before he got to her.

Aching at his protectiveness, intoxicated by his possessiveness, she raised her head and met his wild eyes in the mirrored headboard. The sight of their replicas in the coolness of glass—how he dominated her, how she looked taken whole by him—ignited her down to her last nerve ending. And that was before his words scorched her.

"Five years, Scarlett, five interminable years, struggling with losing you. Now it's even worse, knowing you struggled, too, suffered more." Crying out at the desolation in his voice, she arched back into him, needing to absorb it. "But I have you back now, and you just gave me back every memory I thought I couldn't keep. It was all real. This is real. *This*."

He pressed against her harder, as if he couldn't bear the physical boundaries separating them, his hardness digging into her yielding body. She went limp under him, showing him she wanted him to assimilate her, wanted to dissolve in him.

His eyes kept hers captive, and his hot breath scorched her face, filled her lungs. "I went insane every night, needing you like this and knowing I'd never have you again. Hunger built inside me without even hope for relief."

The first time he'd confessed this, her mind had swerved around his words, shying away from registering them. It was too huge to contemplate that he hadn't had any intimacies since her. This time there was no escaping his meaning. And it was still almost incomprehensible.

Tentatively, she met his gaze in the mirror. "Do you really mean you didn't…didn't…all this time?"

"Yes, I damn well really mean it." He ground harder into her, liquefying her even more. "Since I was a child I achieved absolute control over my urges, to hone my skills. It made me uninterested in sex, especially since I abhorred the form available to me. The Organization provided us with other captives to vent our libidos with."

Their eyes clung, and she knew he must wonder if she'd been one of those captives, if someone he knew had used her for that purpose.

Unable to bear it, she lowered her head to the bed, burying her face in the silk covers, tears starting to pour down her cheeks.

A trembling hand pulled her up to meet his vehement conviction. "I don't care and neither should you. We both did so many things against our will, and we're not responsible for any of it. It doesn't make us less or worse. It actually makes us more and better. We're survivors, conquerors, winners. But you... You're perfect."

Feeling as if her heart had expanded to fill her whole body, she twisted beneath him so hard, she made him roll off her. Then she was all over him, clinging with arms and legs and lips, tears now flowing with gratitude, with relief.

He let her deluge him for a while before taking over, groaning into her lips. "My brothers used to call me The Monk. I thought I was, until you. Then I became insatiable. After you, after I experienced true passion and ecstasy, I couldn't settle for the sexual relief I never wanted in the first place. I wanted you. Only you. Even when I thought I'd never have you again. But now I do, and all I can think of is having you, doing everything to you, with you."

"Everything?" She moaned, undulating against him, needing him to combust. "Like what? Show me."

"Like this…" He flipped her onto her back, gloriously rough, dragging her top over her head and spilling her swollen breasts into the large palms they'd been made to fill. He kneaded them with a careful savagery that had her bucking beneath him, had her frantically trying to tear his clothes off his back. She needed the crush of his hunger, the oblivion of his possession.

Grasping both her hands in one, he did what she'd failed to. He shredded his shirt, flinging off its tatters. Her salivary glands stung, need-ing her lips and tongue all over his flesh, her teeth in it.

"And this." He slid down her body, the velvet of his skin sparking her every inch into a con-flagration. "And this." He nipped each nipple in turn, had her crying out, before settling into suckling that escalated into ruthlessness, had her core pouring, until she was pummeling him for the release only his invasion would grant her.

He escaped her clawing hands, went down far-ther, taking her skirt and panties off with him. "And this."

Holding her feet apart, alternating kisses be-tween them, he suckled her toes, forcing her to withstand the sight and sensations of his ownership, his worship. "And this." He bit into her calves, kneading them with his teeth as he trailed up to her inner thigh, before opening the lips of her core. Tantalizing her, he lapped up the flow of her arousal in long, leisurely licks before growling, "And this." He pinpointed the bud where all her nerves converged, took it in a sharp nip.

The discharge of all the pent-up stimulation

was so explosive, she heaved in detonation after detonation until she felt as if her spine might snap.

He had no mercy. He pushed two fingers inside her, sharpening her pleasure until her voice broke. He didn't stop even then. No, he sucked every spasm and aftershock out of her, blasting her sensitized flesh with more growls. "And this." His thumb circled the swollen nub, had her writhing under the renewed surge, the need for release a rising crest of incoherence.

"Come for me again, my darling."

It was that "my darling" that hurled her into another orgasm.

After he'd finished her, he came up to loom over her, watching her tremble with what he'd done to her, his hand tracing soothing patterns on her back and buttocks. Mute, saturated with pleasure, hungrier for him than ever, she watched him, the emotions on his face coming too fast and thick for her to decipher. To withstand.

Spreading her legs wide, she begged him, "Inside me, Raiden. Come inside me."

He looked down at her, sable hair cascading over his leonine forehead. "I want to be inside you all the time, Scarlett. And I couldn't be for five years. Because you didn't trust me to understand, didn't give me the chance to help you, to protect you, to save you."

Her body contorted under the onslaught of his impassioned upbraiding. "I'm sorry...I didn't think..."

He captured her face in urgent hands. "You thought too much, and all wrong. And you should be sorry. When I think what you almost did to yourself, what you cost us when you kept me in the dark, thinking you were protecting me, my head almost explodes."

"I did protect you," she protested weakly.

"And I want your word you'll never do anything like this again. Never hide anything from me again, Scarlett."

"I won't." She was half lying, for she was still hiding things, but she had to protect him from further pain. Needing to distract him, needing him beyond endurance, she wrapped herself around him. "Don't punish me anymore. Just take me."

His body turned to granite in her arms. "You punished us both when you sacrificed yourself for me. Don't you know I'd rather die than see you hurt? And for you to be hurt on my account… God, I don't know how I'll live with that knowledge."

She stared into his pained eyes, distress expanding in her throat all over again. No, she hadn't known that. She'd never dared dream of anything even far less.

Contrition suffocating her, she needed to take him away from the maddening what-ifs, bring him back to her in this moment. "You're hurting me now, Raiden, making me wait."

It was as if some switch was thrown inside him, the consternation on his face switching to voracity.

In full predator mode, he rose above her, rid himself of his pants and briefs. She felt the usual clench of intimidation at the sight of his girth and length, at his beauty and sleekness. She craved his invasion, not only for the ecstasy it forced from her flesh, but because it was the most intimacy she could have with him.

"Just take me, *please*…."

And he finally did. He rammed inside her,

all his power and the accumulation of frustration and hunger behind the thrust. The head of his erection, nearly too wide for her, rubbed against all the right places, abrading nerves into an agony of response, pushing receptors over the limit of stimuli. Even after the releases he gave her, she was so inflamed that it took only a few unbridled thrusts for her to arch up in a deep bow and scream. In her ecstasy, she saw only his beloved face in focus, clenched in pleasure, his eyes vehement with his greed for her.

Every time with him it got better. Excruciatingly better.

"I can't… Please… You…you… Now…"

He understood, gave her what she needed. The sight of his face seizing, his roars echoing her screams, the feel of him succumbing to the ecstasy she gave him, the hard jets of his climax inside her. They hit her at her peak, had her unable to endure the spike in pleasure, then everything dimmed, faded.…

Heavy breathing and slow heartbeats echoed from the end of a long tunnel as the scents of satisfaction flooded her lungs. Awareness trickled into a body so sated it was numb.

She felt only one thing. Raiden. Still inside her, even harder, larger. She opened lids weighing half a ton each, saw him swim in and out of focus. He was still kneeling between her legs, her buttocks propped on his thighs, her legs around his. One of his palms was kneading her breasts, the other gliding over her shoulders, her arms, her belly.

"You are mine. *Mine.* As Scarlett. As Hannah. As Katya."

She lurched at hearing her real name on his lips. She'd known he must know it now, but hearing him say it…

She moaned as he ground deeper inside her, reaching the point where the familiar expansion turned into almost pain. An edge of dominance that was glorious, addictive, overwhelming, even a little frightening. The idea of all that he was, melding with her, at her mercy as she was at his, filled volumes inside her, body, mind and soul.

"Say it. You're mine. All of you. Every version of you."

"There was only ever one version. The version born to love you."

She truly didn't know what happened after that.

Raiden devoured her, finished her, then did so again and again.

It was as though his passion had always been curbed, but now all his shackles had been broken. He showed her what it could be like with him fully unleashed.

It was beyond description.

After the nightlong conflagration, she lay in his arms in a stupor, every cell in her body overloaded with bliss. At least before the ticking timer inside her resumed the countdown.

Her ten weeks were almost up. No matter what he'd said now, how he felt, his plans were more important, couldn't be changed. And she'd have to exit his life soon.

But she couldn't even contemplate being cut off from him forever.

There was only one way she wouldn't be.

Unsteadily, she struggled to prop herself over his endless chest. Looking down at him, she marveled again that all this beauty and power could be hers, even if temporarily.

Then she made the tentative bid for permanence.

"I want to amend our arrangement, Raiden. I want to remain your lover after you're married."

Eight

Raiden sat up slowly, not only because Scarlett's offer had rocked him to his core, because he felt he'd drained his very life force inside her. Four times.

After that statement, that she'd been born to love him, he didn't know what had happened to him. It was as if every iota of control he'd ever practiced had been building up an opposite wildness, and only a measure of that had been released in the past with her, probably because on some level he'd felt there had been something not quite right. Since they'd been together again, their whole situation had rationed his uninhibitedness. Then she'd made that declaration, and it had been as if the dam inside him had burst.

The way he'd taken her, in a sustained eruption of raging hunger, the way she'd surrendered unconditionally, and the explosive pleasure they'd wrung from each other... It had been transfiguring, transcendent.

After that last time he'd taken her in the shower, he'd taken her back to bed and had been feeling another cataclysm building. Then she'd staggered up and made that out-of-the-blue offer and everything had dissipated with shock.

She was now looking at him avidly, her hair hanging around her gleaming shoulders in thick, wet locks, her lips and body showing the effects of his fierce possession.

He'd never seen anything more beautiful, known anything more overpowering.

The seductive smile playing on her kiss-swollen lips didn't reach her eyes. Those were faltering as she painted his chest in caresses. "Powerful men in Japan almost always have mistresses, and it's accepted as long as they're discreet and don't disgrace their wives and families. I will abide by any precautions you need to maintain our secret." She pouted in a rickety attempt at reprimand. "You'll certainly have to curb the impulses you've been having of late, popping up wherever I am, taking me out or home for all to see."

He suddenly wanted to get up, get away and stop this.

But before he could move, she hugged him fiercely around the waist, laid her hot face over his thudding heart. Her lips trembled against his skin as she spelled out her offer. "If you can't have enough of me, as I can't have enough of you, this doesn't have to end. I don't want to lose you, and I'll do anything, stay anywhere, as long as I can have you like this. I know once you get married your situation will change, but you don't have to leave me behind to have the family, the heritage and the heirs you've planned to have for so long. You can have me indefinitely if you want, and also have everything else you ever craved and deserve."

Raiden's head filled with cacophony, every response that screamed in his mind jumbling together, paralyzing him, muting him.

She was giving him a carte blanche to her life.

It was again the last thing he'd expected. Not that he'd expected anything, being tossed about in last night's tumult.

But if he'd been able to think, he would have come to one conclusion. That it was no longer a possibility he'd give her up on their agreed-on date, or at all. He couldn't even think of a life without her now. Couldn't think of another reason to live but being with her, being hers. He was finally free to face that he'd loved her from the first moment and had never stopped loving her. But he now loved her with a profundity he hadn't thought himself capable of. And he now knew she reciprocated his emotions in full. If he'd thought at all, he would have thought he'd be the one to plead with her not to leave his side.

But she'd preempted him, offering herself without reservations, relegating herself to a permanent position in the shadows in his life.

What hurt most was that she believed it was her natural place, that it was all she was worth, to be hidden as if she was a shameful secret. She believed she was, saw herself as tainted with a stain that would never be cleansed.

Before he voiced one of a million vehement

arguments to the opposite, the color suddenly drained from her face.

"You—you don't want any more time with me, let alone indefinitely, do you?" Her bloodless lips contorted. "It—it's just when you said… I thought you… Oh, God, I'm sorry I—"

Her stumbling apology came to an abrupt end as her eyes rolled back in her head and she sagged back on the bed in a dead faint.

The detonation of terror almost made him follow suit.

He didn't, only because he'd turned to stone with fright.

Then shock splintered and he pounced on her, his heart rupturing. "Scarlett… God, Scarlett, darling…"

She didn't move when he shook her. His hands were shaking so hard, he couldn't detect her pulse….

Stop it. Get yourself under control.

He heard himself barking the self-admonition, tried to force himself to think, but could only think she was lying there, ashen, unmoving. And he couldn't rouse her, couldn't tell if she was breathing.

Yet even panicking, his mechanisms of performing under maximum duress kicked in, making him go through emergency procedures.

Then he did the one thing he'd always done when he or any of his brothers was injured or unwell. He called Antonio.

As soon as the line clicked open, Raiden choked, "Scarlett fainted. I can't wake her up."

Without preamble, Antonio went into doctor mode. "Place her on her back, remove any constricting clothing, raise her legs above heart level about twelve inches, then check her airway for anything blocking it. Watch for vomiting. If she vomits, immediately place her on her side."

"I did all that, and she still won't wake up." His voice barely came out, futile tears starting to run down his cheeks.

"Give me her vitals."

He gritted out her breath and heartbeat count.

"Slow, but not dangerously so. Neurologic status?"

"Reflexes are normal. But she won't wake up!"

"That on its own means nothing. Whatever the reason she's unconscious, she isn't in any immediate danger."

"You can't know that!"

"Given your report, I can. Did you call an ambulance?"

"I called you. You're the best there is. Get your ass over here *now*."

"I assume 'here' is your new residence?" Raiden's apoplectic expletive made Antonio sigh. "Calm down before you give yourself a stroke. I'd rather have only one patient on my hands when I arrive." Before Raiden yelled the building down, he heard slamming doors on the other end of the phone, then before the line went dead, Antonio said, "I'm already on my way."

Shaking out of control, Raiden threw the phone down and pounced on Scarlett. He checked her pulse and breathing over and over, caressed and crooned to her to please wake up.

She didn't. She remained unconscious until Antonio arrived, what felt like an eternity later. It had actually been only ten minutes, which he'd counted second for second. From his perspiring condition, it was clear Antonio had run the whole way from his hotel a few blocks away.

In those endless minutes, Raiden had dressed Scarlett in her underwear, then wrapped her freezing body in the comforter. He'd been wrapped around her to transfer his body heat to her when Steve had let in Antonio. He could now barely relinquish her still form and stand aside to let Antonio start his exam.

Antonio had come prepared, with his magical medical bag as they called it, with supplies and instruments inside ready to handle anything from simple cuts to major field surgery.

He examined Scarlett with all-knowing hands and all-seeing eyes, took her pressure, drew blood, performed neurologic tests, used a few instruments Raiden didn't recognize. Then he finally put everything back into his bag.

Out of his mind by now, Raiden growled like a cornered beast. "Why didn't you wake her up?"

Antonio looked up at him serenely. "Because I can't."

"What do you mean you can't?"

Antonio looked at him with those imperturbable green eyes. "I might be capable of almost anything medically, but contrary to common belief, I can't perform miracles."

"It would take a miracle to wake her up now?" He nearly choked on the words.

"Stop making the worst assumptions, Raiden, for your own health. What you see in movies with instant injections and slaps and smelling salts are just for drama's sake. In the real world you *should* leave an unconscious person to wake up on her own, as long as we've made sure nothing else is wrong with her."

"But there has to be something wrong with her. She just turned off and won't turn back on!"

"I have a diagnosis for that." Antonio stood up, looked him in the eyes like someone about to impart something that would change his life. Then he did. "She's totally exhausted. And seriously upset. *And* certainly pregnant."

Scarlett surfaced from what felt like an abyss.

It had been dark and oppressive down there. But she'd been unwilling to escape it. It had at least been safe, and better than the alternative. That of coming out only to face a far worse bleakness. That of Raiden's rejection.

She'd offered him herself, no strings attached, forever if he'd take her that long. The dismay on his face had hurt so much, she hadn't been able to handle it. She had wished she'd just stop feeling anything so it wouldn't hurt anymore.

She realized she'd fainted. Which was weird. That was the first time her consciousness had given out, yielded to the refuge of oblivion. Not even in her worst of times, and she'd had some nightmarish ones, had it come to her rescue like that. But then, none of those times had been as brutal as knowing it was over with Raiden. Now she was reluctant to exit its protection, wanted to remain in its cold cloak forever.

But there was no use. She was already awake. Even before she opened her eyes, she knew what she'd see. Raiden.

He was standing beside the bed, looking down at her. She could feel his gaze on her, emitting impatience, no doubt for her to come around. There was something else, too. Agitation.

Was that on account of her fainting, or of the offer she'd made before she had? Or both? Did he think he'd have a hysterical female on his hands once she woke up? One who'd start clinging and causing him problems he couldn't afford?

Might as well open her eyes and reassure him

that he had nothing to fear from her. She'd made a desperate bid for more time with him, and she'd lost. As she'd known she would. But she'd had to try. Now it was over, and she'd go in silence as she'd intended. But he didn't know that. It was time to let him know.

She opened her eyes, and his image filled her aching gaze. He'd put on pants, was standing over her like a monolith, every muscle in his majestic body bunched, making him look even more perfect, more intimidating. That body that had owned and pleasured hers in magical ways would soon be only a memory. Just like everything else with him. Even his confession that he'd been with no other woman. No matter how he desired her, his plans were what mattered to him. As they should.

Struggling to prop herself up, she pushed hair out of her eyes. "Sorry for passing out on you like that."

"How can you apologize? It isn't as if you could have done something about it."

He sounded hoarse. She did, too, her voice abused with too many cries of pleasure. It felt so strange, made her feel so cold, after that indescribable interlude of intimacy, for him to be standing there, separate from her. But she'd known all along that this was coming. Maybe this fainting spell had been timely, ending the scene she would have so impulsively caused. Now discussing it would be without the flagrant emotions of the moment, would be distant and detached.

She sat up. "I guess not. But I do apologize for what I said before I fainted. It must have been the euphoric high after the incredible sex. But I'm taking back everything I said and we're returning to our scheduled separation. In fact, I think I just pushed the date forward. We had the revelations and confessions and got everything out in the open and off our chests, and had an unprecedented session worthy of a last hurrah. Anything after that would be redundant, so it's time to say our goodbyes."

She flung the comforter off as if it burned her, even if it acutely dismayed her to be semi-naked in front of him now. Now that their intimacies were over, she felt as she had all her life, stripped of her every dignity and hiding place. She felt far worse than she ever had. With any other, she hadn't cared about feeling like a sullied, expendable object.

She talked as she started to dress. "I'm leaving Japan within a week. So it will be before your wedding. This time when I disappear, you won't have to worry you'll ever see me again."

"Was that the original plan? To disappear without telling me?"

She blinked up at him. His face was gripped in some emotion she couldn't fathom. Every angle in his masterpiece bone structure jutted out more against his burnished skin, as if he was straining under an insupportable burden.

"Telling you what?"

"That you're pregnant."

If Raiden had told her he was an alien, then flew around the room to prove it, she wouldn't have been more stunned.

She must have gaped at him for minutes before she closed her open mouth and tried to overcome her shock.

"When were you going to tell me, Scarlett?"

Slowly, carefully, as if testing her voice for the first time, she said, "Never, I guess. Since I'm not."

His eyes suddenly took on a faraway look. "I *have* been feeling it in every inch of you. The changes in your body, in your appetite, the extra sensitivity to some scents, to my touch. But I didn't reach the obvious conclusion, because I thought you'd tell me if it was true. But you didn't." His eyes focused on hers again, something enormous roiling in their depths. "Why, Scarlett? Was it because you thought we'd say goodbye and I didn't have to know?" His face drained of all color suddenly. "Or was it because it was a mistake, one you intended to…fix?"

She shook her head, his every word making her more nauseous. "If you're suspecting I fainted because I'm pregnant, don't. I can't be."

"Why can't you be? I haven't taken any precautions."

She raised her hands, needing to stop this before she fainted again, or vomited, or both. "You didn't because you assumed I did. So if you're thinking you shouldn't have left this in my hands, that if I'm pregnant it would cause you major trouble, don't be. I am *not* pregnant."

It was his turn to gape at her. "You're really not aware that you are pregnant, are you?"

"Listen, Raiden, I'm not only not pregnant, I *can't* be pregnant. So stop it...*please.*"

"What do you mean *can't?* You are."

"No, I'm not." He opened his mouth to persist, and her voice rose to a shriek to drown out his. "I can't *ever* be pregnant. I had a traumatic miscarriage and doctors told me I'd never be able to get pregnant again!"

Raiden staggered a step back. Even the most innocuous words from Scarlett hit him harder than any of the vicious blows he'd had in his life, literal or figurative. But this blow almost felled him, when nothing before had ever even compromised his balance.

She truly had no idea she was pregnant. She thought she couldn't become pregnant. Because she'd...she'd...

It made sense, explained the pervasive loss in her eyes that not even her past or their present situation explained. That was what he'd still felt her holding back from him. And he had to heal that wound that remained open inside her.

"You were pregnant with my child?" He made it a question, in case it hadn't been his. She hadn't given a time frame, and it might have happened long before they'd met. Even though everything inside him screamed she'd lost his—their—baby.

From the wounded look in her eyes, his care seemed to offend her. "You think I would have let myself get pregnant by another man? Protecting myself was the first thing I was taught in the business I was pushed into."

His heart squeezed and expanded at the same time. Her pregnancy had been premeditated. Out loud he still asked, "You let yourself become pregnant with my child?"

She looked away, as if she could no longer bear looking at him. "I knew there was no possible future with you, but I wanted to at least have a part of you with me always. I had this plan that I was going to save you from Medvedev, escape The Organization and go somewhere safe and raise the baby on my own, give it the life we've both been robbed of. But we both know how this plan went."

Was it possible there was always more pain? He felt a new level of agony contemplating the incredible courage and selflessness and love it took to make those plans. It was excruciating imagining how she'd felt—the resignation that she'd never have him, the hope she'd considered the epitome of her ambitions, the determination to have a baby, alone, make it safe and loved, as she'd never been.

He struggled not to sag to his knees before her, not to beg her to forgive him for not being there for her, for being oblivious, for not giving her everything she deserved. He choked out his words. "It went spectacularly for the most part. You did save me from Medvedev, did escape The Organization."

"Not because my plan was masterful or anything. The one reason I pulled it off and I'm not dead is because Medvedev underestimated me and underestimated what I'd do to protect you. It was all touch and go and the price was our—" Her face seized, as if she'd caught herself in a terrible faux pas. "The baby. Now I'm unable to have any other."

Before he insisted she'd always call it "our baby," before he convinced her she was already having another one, there was one more poison he needed her to purge from her system. "It was Medvedev's stab that aborted our baby."

Her throat worked as she nodded, confirming his statement, her face that impassive mask he now realized she'd tailored to obscure enormous emotions and suffering.

"They told me it was the baby that saved my life, taking most of the damage for me. But the damage to my uterus was too extensive. They told me I'd never have children again."

He was unable to find words to express his pain and regret and rage and frustration that he couldn't change the past, couldn't give of his own life and flesh to defend hers, to wipe away her scars, mental and physical. And that he couldn't punish Medvedev a thousand times over. But he promised himself again he'd punish everyone who had a hand in Medvedev's existence, and in her suffering, past and present.

But now he had to dispel at least one of her agonies.

Producing the proof from his pocket, he took her hand and placed it in her palm. "This is a blood-testing chip that our resident medical genius in Black Castle Enterprises has patented.

He says it yields one hundred percent results in diagnosing a variety of conditions, one of which is pregnancy. He came to my rescue when you fainted and performed the blood test, and his diagnosis is unequivocal. You *are* pregnant."

Scarlett dazedly looked down at the credit card–size transparent plastic chip. The slot for HCG, the hormone detecting pregnancy, was a bright positive red.

Shaking her head, she raised disbelieving eyes to him. "It must be a mistake. I—I can't be pregnant."

"Antonio doesn't make mistakes, Scarlett. The ones who made a mistake were the doctors who gave you that verdict." When she shook her head again, she swayed and he surged to steady her, taking her by the shoulders. "We'll redo the test just to put your mind to rest. But we always trusted Antonio with our very lives. If he's certain, so am I. He believes you're eight weeks pregnant."

Still shaking her head, looking punch-drunk, Scarlett whispered, "That's how long ago our first night was."

Poignancy tightened his hands, bringing her

beloved body closer. "I do have a feeling you got pregnant that night."

Tears suddenly welled in her reddened eyes, then flowed down her cheeks, cutting streaks into his heart. "But I saw the CT scans. The damage was too extensive. Even if I'm pregnant…it can't be possible I'll carry the baby to term. Or it's even worse, and it's an ectopic pregnancy. That would still yield a positive test result."

The thought that she could be right about either possibility gripped his heart in crushing dread. He ran to call Antonio.

At his barked order to come back at once, Antonio only asked if Scarlett was awake. Raiden affirmed that, and Antonio only told him to put him on speaker.

Vibrating with anxiety, Raiden complied, though he didn't know why he'd asked that. Antonio was a prankster, but he wouldn't tease him about something like this, and certainly not now of all times.

Once on speaker, Antonio addressed Scarlett. "I assume you didn't realize you're pregnant? Because you thought it wasn't possible?" Scarlett looked even more dazed that Antonio knew what both of them hadn't known. "And now that you do, you're worried about the viability of your pregnancy? And that's why Raiden is working on a stroke again?"

After Scarlett nodded weakly as if Antonio could see her, Antonio went on as if he had. "I can see why you thought that. I performed a thorough exam with ultrasound, but Raiden must have been too agitated to notice, or he didn't recognize my patented handheld ultrasound for what it is. I did see your old scars, inside and out, and from their site and extensiveness, I can see why your doctors would have given you a prognosis of sterility. And they would have been absolutely right, if not for something exceptional about you.

"You're one of a rare percentage blessed with no scarring tendencies. This means your wounds heal almost as elastic as your intact tissues and skin. It's why your esthetic surgery is virtually undetectable. From the current condition of your uterus, I believe you'll carry your baby without incident and with normal activity to at least thirty-two weeks. After that, I recommend bed rest until term. Your miracle baby's development is above average, and you'll surely do everything so it continues to grow at the same rate, so by thirty-six weeks it should be mature enough to be delivered. I recommend C-section, which I'll of course perform."

After Antonio finished his thorough medical report, he promised he'd allocate her a whole day for a total checkup. He suffered Raiden's over-whelmed, overwhelming thanks and ended the call because he was in the middle of surgery.

She remained staring at Raiden all through, her face a mask of shock. Then suddenly the mask cracked and the whole spectrum of emo-tions fast-forwarded on her face. What she'd just learned, what she'd long craved and despaired of, coming true so unexpectedly… It must be changing everything inside her, rearranging her life and expectations forever. As it was his.

Not that the pregnancy changed what he felt, or what he intended to do. His love for her had al-ready changed everything. The pregnancy, espe-cially one thought to be impossible, was just an extra jubilation. And it was the least fate owed her after all she'd overcome, all she was doing to spare others what she'd suffered.

And it would be only the beginning. She'd have love and safety and cherishing and everything that he was and had to give for the rest of his life.

"Raiden…" She swayed again, and he caught her, swept her up in a fervent embrace and took her back to bed.

He knew she fell asleep the moment she touched the sheets. It had all been too much for her. But now it wasn't a dead faint that claimed her, but deep, recharging sleep. The heartbreakingly blissful smile on her lips said that.

All he wanted was to strip both of them and fuse their flesh and go to sleep wrapped around her, enfolding her and their coming baby in his love and protection.

But before he did that, his phone rang.

Thinking it must be Antonio calling back to add medical advice, he eagerly and not a little anxiously answered.

"Raiden-san, you must come to my office at once."

His uncle's clipped command shot through him with dismay.

The call was over the moment he said, "Of course." Whatever his uncle had to say, he would say only to his face.

In the next second, a smile played on his lips. He marveled at how everything was conspiring to come together. Numair's discoveries had led to Scarlett's confessions, then to Antonio's revelation. Now, from his usually courteous uncle's coldness, this was leading to the confrontation Raiden had been expecting. But instead of placating his uncle and taking a slap on his wrist for his public indiscretions with Scarlett the past two weeks, he'd inform his uncle he was no longer his future father-in-law.

In half an hour, he entered his uncle's office, found him standing behind his desk, leaning on it, palms down. From his wiped-clean-of-expression face, and that he didn't meet him at the door and didn't salute him now, Raiden knew the man was furious.

Good. It would make this easier. It was always

harder giving people their marching orders when they were nice.

Takeo Hashimoto started without preamble. "We've found out about your illicit relationship with that foreign woman."

Just as he'd figured. He was even wondering why this confrontation hadn't happened earlier.

Raiden regarded his uncle calmly as he took a seat across his desk. It was regretful Hashimoto would not become family. He'd been starting to feel he was truly his flesh and blood. But this was probably the last time he'd see the man. Or if he saw him again, it would be as antagonists, at least on Hashimoto's side. Breaking his honor-bound pact would be an irreparable insult. There was no coming back from that.

"We? You mean you've told Megumi?"

"She's the one who told me."

That surprised Raiden. Not that Megumi knew, for of course she'd have been the first to be made aware of his indiscretions. But he hadn't thought she of all people would care, let alone run to her father with the information.

"It was that mongrel Hiro Matsuyama who set

this up. And now he claims this woman carries your child."

This straight-out flabbergasted Raiden. Had *everyone* realized Scarlett was pregnant before they did?

But he asked his uncle the question relevant to him. "What does Hiro have to do with any of this?"

Hashimoto looked at him as if he'd dropped a hundred points of his IQ. "He brought her to that ball, where he pretended to honor your and Megumi's engagement. But he only did so he'd put that professional seductress in your way."

Dread zapped through Raiden. Was it possible Hashimoto had found out about Scarlett's past identity? No. He couldn't have. But why would he say that about her if he didn't?

Sitting forward, he picked his words with care. "She's a humanitarian worker, and she's Hiro's best friend. How did you come up with the theory that Hiro threw her in my path so she'd seduce me? Why would Hiro want that anyway?"

"Because he covets Megumi," Hashimoto barked. "He not only wants to stop your marriage, but he needs to do it with a scandal big enough that the ensuing disgrace would make it impossible for us to aspire to another worthy match. Then I'd be forced to accept someone like him as a husband for her."

This was yet another surprise. Raiden hadn't detected that Hiro was attracted to Megumi. But then, in the only time he'd seen them together, he'd been busy thinking that Hiro was besotted with Scarlett.

But now that he replayed that ball in his mind, he could see the whole thing in a new light. Hiro's aggression toward him had been over Megumi. And Megumi's agitation had been over Hiro.

Those two were in love!

That must be why Megumi had told her father about him and Scarlett. So he'd break off the engagement and she'd be free to be with Hiro.

God, how blind had he been?

But at least no real damage had been done. He'd call Hiro after he broke things off with his uncle, telling him to rush to make a huge bid while the man was most open to compensatory offers. Even from someone he considered socially abhorrent.

For his uncle's sake, Raiden hoped he'd accept Hiro right away. His snobbery, though socially dictated, was starting to grate. If he exercised it on Hiro now that he realized there was mutual love involved, he'd show him his displeasure. He was sure his uncle wouldn't like to see his displeased side.

"So you just found out?" he asked.

"Megumi first told me three weeks after the ball."

Raiden's eyebrows shot up. That far back? The only way Megumi could have found out when he'd still been discreet was through Hiro. Being close to Scarlett, he must have noticed her sudden change of schedule, and all the other telltale signs of a woman being regularly, ferociously loved. Hiro could have also had a report of their garden house meeting and put one and one together. Maybe he'd even followed them to cement his deductions. As for how he'd realized Scarlett was pregnant, she did have all the signs for someone who was looking.

He sighed. "What kept you silent all this time?"

Hashimoto's dignified face darkened with disapproval. "At first you were discreet, and I thought you'd indulge in this woman for a while before settling down to a life of respectability with my pure daughter. Then you started getting careless, letting our partners and rivals see you flaunting that loose woman everywhere, taking her home with you for all to see. It's two weeks away from your wedding and I'm sure I just pulled you out of that woman's arms."

Raiden sighed again. "Yes, you just did."

"Is it also right you've impregnated her?"

The idea that hadn't sunk in fully yet, of Scarlett carrying his baby, a miracle baby by all accounts, spread his lips with its intense delight. "That is absolutely right."

Hashimoto looked at him in such horror, as if he'd just watched him cut off his own arm. "Don't you realize the magnitude of scandal this will cause?"

Raiden nodded calmly. "It won't be as bad as you think."

If he'd married Megumi, then had an illegitimate child with Scarlett, that would have been the stuff of permanent social stigma for the Hashimotos. But breaking off the engagement, even at this late date, for his pregnant gaijin lover… That would only be the stuff of malicious gossip. The most the Hashimotos would suffer would be a period of social ridicule. As for Raiden, he'd leave Japan, never to return. His exit from the scene would soon douse the scandal.

"Raiden-san, I truly expected better from you, far better. I never suspected you'd be so gullible that a woman like that could trick you into such a catastrophic position."

He pursed his lips. It was time to put him straight and end this. "Ms. Delacroix is a noble, courageous and benevolent woman, Takeo-sama, and I won't allow even a hint of disrespect toward her. She is the woman I love, the mother of my future child and the one I'm going to marry."

Hashimoto now looked as if Raiden had hacked off *his* arm.

Raiden exhaled forcibly. "I truly hoped we'd be family, Takeo-sama. I would have been honored to be your adopted son. But this will ultimately be for the best. I'm sorry I didn't end this earlier, but circumstances dictated the timing. You beat me to this confrontation, but the result would have been the same no matter who instigated it."

Hashimoto sagged down to his chair as if Raiden had shot him between the eyes. "You can't do this, Raiden-san… You can't. I—I called you here to demand you end your liaison right away, send that woman…" At his warning glance, Hashimoto swallowed. "Send Ms. Delacroix out of Japan."

"And now you know why I came to see you."

"But even if you no longer care about entering our family, or about destroying our honor, there are billions at stake. For everyone. And everyone includes Yakuza bosses."

This brought Raiden to the edge of his seat. "What the hell are you talking about?"

"Did you think a merger of this magnitude can happen without them insinuating themselves in it for a sizable piece of the pie? There are a dozen Yakuza branches counting on you becoming the head of our family, once this marriage comes through, *and* remains solid and producing heirs. But thanks to your lack of discretion, they found out about your liaison with Ms. Delacroix and were worried."

Before Raiden said everyone could go to hell for all he cared, Hashimoto drove his point home. "They are waiting like vultures for the mergers to occur so they'd have their commissions. They were already considering intervention to put an end to your liaison when they had no doubt you'd still marry Megumi. If they find out you won't, Ms. Delacroix will become an obstacle in the path of their interests. They wouldn't think twice about removing her from yours...permanently."

Nine

Raiden stared down at the city of Tokyo, sizzling with light and nightlife, his uproar ratcheting with every breath.

Unable to bear looking down anymore on this city where he'd once felt an intense sense of belonging, he closed the automatic blinds and crossed the penthouse in the dark.

Not that he needed lights. He'd operated in darkness more than half his life. He'd needed nothing but his skills, his will and his brothers. To succeed, to excel, to survive.

To live, he needed only Scarlett.

Everyone kept telling him he couldn't have her. His brothers, his uncle, society. All these didn't matter. Their opinions could be either changed or disregarded.

The Yakuza mattered. Their opinion was unchangeable.

And they'd sent him his uncle with a simple message.

Get rid of Scarlett, or they will.

He'd thought he'd once known fear, as a helpless child in the hands of monsters. He hadn't experienced its acrid taste since he'd become part of his brotherhood, had long forgotten the sensation. But he'd never known what fear really felt like. Now he knew. Fearing for her safety was unadulterated, sanity-destroying dread.

His uncle had told him he wouldn't make public Raiden's intention to cancel the wedding and to marry Scarlett instead. Not until Raiden decided how to handle the Yakuza's threat. Though he'd been angry and upset that Raiden had reneged on his promises, he was more worried about him.

When Raiden, murderously angry, had told him he could protect himself and his own, his uncle had made valid arguments to the contrary.

The Yakuza needed an ongoing merger to reap

the benefits, the kind that came only from stable marriages and legitimate heirs. They'd already bought stock and placed bets depending on the marriage that wouldn't come to pass. His relationship with Scarlett had already hurt their business, but they probably hadn't removed her nuisance already since they expected Raiden to do as he was told, and they'd rather not alienate him unnecessarily. But if they thought they were losing him anyway, they'd have nothing at risk. Eliminating Scarlett would serve as a punishment to him, and a cautionary tale to anyone else who didn't abide by their rules.

He'd sworn to his uncle he would kill them all first.

His uncle had only looked at him as if he'd lost his mind. Then he'd told him he'd do everything in his power to mollify them, to buy him time, until Raiden got his act together.

Even in his maddened wrath, Raiden had known that his uncle was right. Killing them all wasn't a viable option.

He alone could eliminate a dozen Yakuza heads before the night was out. Enlisting his brothers' help would widen his preemptive strikes by a factor of six. But there was no way they'd get everyone. The Yakuza were a cancer. Remove the main tumors and others sprouted in their place. There would be retaliatory hits sooner or later. Apart from keeping Scarlett hidden indefinitely, or changing her identity all over again, she'd always be in danger. Even if he disappeared with her, that still left his brothers. The Yakuza didn't forget their vendettas, needed to demonstrate their lessons viciously to keep their future quarries in line. When their original target escaped them, they forced the target to surface by hitting at their nearest and dearest. If that didn't work, they'd at least made an example that would ensure no one crossed them again.

No. Neither striking first nor hiding was the answer. Too much was at stake. Everything was at stake.

Scarlett was everything.

Keeping her and their baby safe required a different mode of attack. And for that, he needed his brothers. All of them. This had to be planned with no margin of error. None.

He entered his pitch-dark bedroom, knowing without needing to see that Scarlett was still out on his bed like the lights. Her scent enveloped him; her essence permeated him.

Doing what he'd wanted to do before his fateful meeting with his uncle, he stripped, joined her on the bed, rid her of her own clothes and cocooned her in his body, as if he'd taken her inside him, where she'd be totally safe.

He had to rest now, while she did.

Tomorrow a war began.

Raiden woke up the moment she did.

Keeping his eyes closed and his body relaxed, he hid the fact that he was awake, too. He needed her to go about her daily business as if nothing was different. The Yakuza would be watching both him and her more closely now that they'd sent their message. Yet he couldn't alarm or distress her a moment before he had to. It already killed him that he would soon have to.

He lay there on his side as she separated her precious flesh from his, as she'd been doing every morning, gently, careful not to disturb him. Then as if she couldn't help herself, she pressed back to him for a moment, feathering his chest with kisses. His heart almost imploded.

Pretending to turn in his sleep so she wouldn't feel it thundering against her chest, he separated from her. A tiny sigh escaped her, a blissful little sound, as she placed a final kiss over his shoulder, then left the bed.

In the fifteen minutes it took her to get ready to leave, he almost suffocated with a dozen conflicting urges. To drag her back to bed and drown in her, to grab her and run out of Japan and disappear, to tell her everything now, not later. But the main need remained to go out and take down as many of those who threatened her as possible. A need he knew would go unfulfilled. But he still swore he was adding those goons to his list of undetectable and unendurable punishments.

But her safety came first, and last.

As she exited the bedroom, he thought he heard her humming a song. His heart stopped to make sure he'd heard right, before it rocketed into a whole new level of turmoil. She'd never done anything so spontaneous around him. He'd never heard her sound so…cheerful. For the first time in her life, he believed she was happy.

And he'd soon have to mar that happiness.

The moment the penthouse door clicked closed behind her, he exploded from bed. In minutes, he'd set off the general alarm, set up a meeting with those of his brothers still in Japan, with the others joining them on videoconference.

He needed a solution before this day was over. And he *would* have it.

"Which Yakuza bosses made this threat?"

That was Numair, as usual the first one who spoke up with the most relevant question or comment after one of them made a report on a problem they were gathered to resolve.

Raiden had made his investigations. He now knew where the threat was coming from. He told his brothers.

All of them had intimate knowledge of every figure of power in the world, from heads of state to criminal masterminds. The names he'd just mentioned were among the most vicious.

After a minute of silence, Richard was the first to talk. "Are you sure you want to antagonize those vipers? You Japanese people have this weird obsession with honor and ritual, your vendettas last centuries and it makes your criminals the most tenacious on the planet."

Raiden turned to hold the Englishman's gaze. "I wouldn't only antagonize the very devil for Scarlett, I'd die for her and take down anyone with me. But that's why I gathered you all, to find another way that doesn't include antagonizing them. I want this done gracefully and faultlessly, to ensure no fallout of any kind, ever."

"I'm missing something, it seems."

This was Jakob Wolff, their resident Norse god, as the media called him and as all women agreed. Having been given the codename Brainiac during their years with The Organization, he'd turned his weaponry and tech virtuosity into an R&D division that produced the next level of technology, probably Black Castle's highest grossing. He and Raiden had always had their...differences.

Jakob now looked out of the screen at him, his steel-hued eyes boring into Raiden's. "I assume when you say you'd take down anyone with you, that includes us? And we should agree to that, why?"

Raiden shot him a glance in lieu of a *kakato-*

geri ax kick over his thick head. "Because you *owe* Scarlett your fortunes, your security and your very lives. Medvedev uncovered my identity and by association yours, and was coming after all of us. She almost sacrificed her own life taking him down. That's why."

Jakob met his infuriated gaze in utmost composure. "Now, that's a good reason. I thought you expected us to do that for you. My bad."

"Shut up, Brainiac."

Numair's silky command got a dismissive grunt from Jakob. But he did break off the visual duel with Raiden. Numair would always remain their commander. They'd entrusted their lives to him when they'd been children, and no matter how they changed or how powerful they grew, they'd always take orders from him, and he would always have the last say.

"What do you need us to do, Raiden?"

That was Rafael, probably his closest brother, and the one Raiden had been reluctant to call, since he was a newlywed with a baby on the way, too. Raiden hadn't wanted to take him from Eliana's side. After that memorable encounter with her before their wedding in Brazil, where they'd settled down, he had a permanent soft spot for Rafael's bride. Eliana was also just the kind of friend he wanted for Scarlett.

"I want you to use every resource and connection at your disposal, call in all your favors and practice every pressure tactic to make sure it's in the Yakuza's best interests to forget Scarlett exists."

Rafael was the one who nodded immediately. Raiden could see the others thinking of the logistics of his demand, wheels turning in their heads as they planned its execution.

Not that he even considered any of them would reject him. He knew they'd do all they could to help him. But he had to leave them in no doubt how grave the situation was.

"If I can't be assured of her total and permanent security, I won't only relinquish my identity and fake my death and hers, like we did before, but when we resurface, to make sure all of us remain safe from retaliations, I won't even tell you as whom. You'll never see me again."

"And how can any of us live without your aggravation, Lightning?" That was Ivan, his tone teasing, but his eyes alarmed, unable to contemplate losing another of their own. Like they'd lost Cypher.

Richard added his vote. "You and Rafael are the only reason I put up with this group of weasels and your moose of a leader. I'd do anything to keep you around, lad."

Richard's comment was met with generalized snorts, before each man followed with his own pledge in his own way.

"Losing one of us, even pains in the neck—" Numair's gaze singled out Jakob "—or extra baggage—" his gaze flicked to Richard "—is never an option." He stopped, no doubt remembering how they'd lost one of their brothers before, and hadn't been able to do anything about it. Cypher had disappeared without a trace. They all carried guilt that would never go away for their roles in his loss. Numair exhaled. "As for your beloved…"

"She's my *everything.*" Raiden interjected forcefully. "And now she's giving me even more than that. She's carrying our miracle child."

Looking gratefully again at Antonio, the one who'd given him the best news of his life, he explained what made their baby such a miracle.

His brothers took a minute to digest the new info before they bombarded him with their teasing and congratulations.

He allowed himself those moments to accept yet another form of his brothers' support, his heart stuttering at realizing he was beginning to feel like a proud—and insanely anxious—father.

Then came Numair's summation, the decree they'd all abide by. "We would have scorched the earth for Scarlett, just because she's yours. But now we know she almost sacrificed herself for you, and us by association, and we know what she suffered because of her sacrifice, what it almost cost her, and you, anyone daring to threaten her will pay. Long after they back down." Numair looked around, getting corroborating nods from everyone. Nodding in turn, he drummed his fingers on the arm of his chair as he sat forward, as he used to when a direction was settled and it was time to drum out details. "Now let's see how we'll make the Yakuza offer to guard Scarlett and your baby with their lives, for life."

For the next three hours they discussed every detail and possibility, and came up with a plan.

Then Ivan and Antonio left, and the others signed out of the videoconference, each going to initiate his part in the tapestry of manipulation.

Numair stayed behind a few minutes longer to make sure Raiden wouldn't postpone the first thing he had to do.

Pain crushed his heart as he conceded the necessity of that action. It was the hardest thing Raiden would ever do. Giving the Yakuza what they were now waiting for.

And he had to make it look convincing.

The first thing Scarlett noticed as she walked into the downtown office was the avid looks everyone gave her.

She'd already been drawing extreme interest since Raiden had first come for her here. And that was before they'd learned who the god who regularly swept her away in his chariot was.

But now they were making no attempt to hide that they were talking about her. Gossip was a paramount pastime around here, even more than anywhere else in the world she'd been, and she'd already been the subject of the mandatory form, as a gaijin who looked the way she did. But now she couldn't understand the reason for their sudden in-your-face nosiness.

She didn't wonder long. Finding Hiro waiting for her in her office explained everything.

Hiro was the second billionaire who'd come for her in as many weeks. Not only that, but she'd recently learned he was one who was considered a hero of the people, a man who had left his father's path in crime and made himself into a major power in Japan out of nothing. And while it was common knowledge they were friends, her colleagues had only heard about this, as they always met outside of their respective workplaces. For him to be here must be the stuff of folktales to them.

She was happy to see him as usual, and just truly, deliriously *happy* for the first time in her life. Her lips spread wide as she rushed toward him. Deciding to give her openly watching colleagues more to gossip about, no doubt all over the cyberspace everyone here practically lived in, she hugged him exuberantly. She thought a few took photos.

She pulled away, still holding Hiro by the arms. "To what do I owe this wonderful surprise?"

"You won't think it wonderful when you know why I'm here."

It was then she noticed his pained expression, her delight turning to concern. "Is something wrong with you? With Megumi?"

Hiro gave a difficult nod. "There is something terribly wrong. Something she and I are guilty of."

"For God's sake, Hiro, just tell me what it is."

Looking as if he'd choke on guilt, Hiro stood with shoulders slumped. "That night of the ball, one of my guards told me he saw you and Kuroshiro arriving at the garden house one after the other. Afterward, you were…different, and I just knew it was because of him. So I followed you. The moment I became certain that the two of you had something going on, I told Megumi."

She gaped at him. That was out of left field. She'd never suspected *he* suspected a thing. Went to show how totally blinded by Raiden she was. She was unable to see anything but him.

She sighed, led him to her couch, pulled him down with her. "You wanted Megumi to break the engagement."

"There *is* no engagement. He's seen her exactly five times in the past nine weeks and never alone. He's with *you* all the time. But when she told her father that, he told her it's expected that men like Raiden would have a mistress."

She winced at the word *mistress,* and the fact that now Megumi's father, the man who'd become Raiden's adoptive father, knew about her. But from his nonchalant reaction, it meant Raiden had known what he was doing when he'd started being open about their affair. He'd realized his uncle wouldn't care, that it wouldn't jeopardize his marriage adoption. As she hoped nothing would.

She hadn't given it any thought in the tumult of last night, but now she did. She knew her pregnancy would change nothing, nor did she want it to.

But maybe Hiro had just delivered the best news. If Raiden's uncle didn't care, maybe she could remain in Raiden's life as she'd suggested before her pregnancy had been discovered and the subject had been dropped. She could be with him at least until she started to show. Having a mistress was one thing; having a pregnant one was another. One of the main reasons he was getting married was to have heirs—the legitimate kind. An illegitimate child would be a problem to any man, as illegitimacy was a huge issue here. But for someone in Raiden's sensitive position, being so newly added to such a noble family register, it would be untenable.

But no matter what happened, it was enough for her to be carrying his baby. *His baby.*

The fireworks of disbelief and jubilation went off in her blood again.

She'd been shocked, then incredulous, then so frantically elated, she'd shut down again, unable to handle the surge of hope and happiness. Becoming pregnant had been so impossible in her mind, she'd disregarded all the very definite signs of pregnancy she'd been having. But what had been the height of her hopes in the past, and what she'd long given up on, had really come to pass. Antonio might consider it was a physical fluke about her that made this pregnancy possible, and far better, viable, but she preferred to think her love for Raiden had healed all her scars. She also thought maybe fate had finally seen fit to make it up to her, with a miracle whose joy would erase everything she'd ever suffered.

"Scarlett?"

She blinked, and Hiro's worried face filled her vision.

She'd melted back on the couch as she'd continued her giddy musings. And *giddy* also described her physical state. She must be looking as dizzy and nauseous as she felt. She hoped she didn't vomit in Hiro's presence. Again. She'd done so last week and had thought she was coming down with something, had even made the oblivious comment then.

She struggled to sit up. "Sorry for zonking out on you like that. Seems that bug I caught is tenacious."

"I know you're pregnant, Scarlett."

Her smile froze and her mouth dropped open.

"I've seen all the signs during the past two weeks. You vomited, you couldn't bear the scent of my aftershave though I didn't change it, nothing tasted the same to you and your perception of warmth and cold had nothing to do with the actual weather."

She shook her head, stunned. "Wow, you sure know your pregnancy signs and symptoms."

"I have sisters and ten nephews and nieces. I know everything there is to know about pregnancy."

"I guess there's no point in denying it. But I can trust you to keep my secret, right?" She elbowed him playfully.

"Actually, you can't."

Her mouth hung wide again. "Huh?"

"That's what I'm here to confess." Hiro's agitation ratcheted with every word. "I wanted to expose Raiden, to corner him into doing the right thing by Megumi and by you. I went to Megumi's father with my discovery, and I was…loud. I think everyone in his office heard me. It was long after I left that I realized I'd exposed you, too, and betrayed your trust. I still hoped nothing would come of it. Then I woke up this morning and saw it, rushed here to at least explain before you did."

Her heart seemed to hold its beat. "Saw what?"

"The news of your pregnancy all over the newspapers and the internet."

It had been two hours since Hiro had left. She was still sitting where he'd left her. All she'd done since had been reaching for her tablet to check the tabloids.

And it *was* all there, complete with a thorough photo documentation of all of her appearances with Raiden. The feverishly gossipy articles dissected their torrid affair, and ended with the speculation she'd been having about the possibilities in their future, just in outlandish versions. One article hypothesized that Raiden would convert to a religion that would legally allow him to practice bigamy.

All in all, it was an unqualified disaster.

And its shock waves must have reached Raiden by now.

In fact, it must have reached him long before now. So why hadn't he contacted her? She had to see him at once to figure—

"Scarlett."

Raiden. Here. As if she'd summoned him.

She turned her head so suddenly, the world spun again and she slumped back on the couch. He rushed from the wide-open door and swooped down on her, looking exactly as she imagined herself to look. Harassed, unsteady and nauseous.

Not that he could be physically nauseous as she was, but he must be sick to his stomach with the developments.

Before she could say anything, apologize for the trouble this would cause him, he caught her head in both his large hands, hitting her like his namesake with an enervating bolt of craving. He claimed her lips in a devouring kiss that mimicked his latest overriding possession.

She'd become a puddle of longing by the time he pulled back to sear her in the roiling emotions radiating from his gaze and every pore of his body. Then he spoke, and every supporting impulse in her body gave way.

Catching her in a fierce embrace, he repeated what he'd just said, every word expanding inside her until she felt she'd burst with the enormity of it all.

"I love you, Scarlett. I've always loved you, and I will love you to the day I die."

He'd said it again and again before she could at last vent a measure of her shock. "Oh, God, Raiden…you do?"

"What did you think our magical five months were about? And the five years I didn't even think of having another woman? And the past miraculous eight weeks, with their heaven-sent outcome?"

"I—I didn't think, I just loved you, just wanted to love you…and loved every second with you."

"You didn't know I loved you in the past? You didn't feel me working up to ask you to be with me forever?"

"I—I thought you loved Hannah, who didn't exist."

He ran his fingers through her hair, his eyes a blaze of sincerity. "I only ever saw *you,* whatever name you used or whatever facade you wore. You admitted that you were always yourself with me, and I already told you it was you I felt, you I wanted. But I never confessed completely. Now I am confessing. I will never again hide an iota of what I feel for you. I love you. I worship every breath you take. You're everything to me, my darling, everything. You and our miracle child."

She closed her eyes, wanting to trap that image of him as he looked at her with his whole being, the tremor of truth vibrating through all of him, as he confessed his equal and total involvement.

Then she opened her eyes and she felt as if she'd been born again. Born to a world where she didn't have to be alone, but had the love of the only person she'd ever loved with everything in her, with all of her past and future, her strengths and scars.

"Now I want you to do something for me," he said. "Without questions."

She grabbed his hands, her heart ricocheting in her chest with alarm at the darkness that tinged his face and voice. "You know I'd do anything for you."

"I want you to leave Japan. Today. I want you to pack your essentials and go back to the States. I'll pack everything else for you once you give me an address to send it to."

She gaped at him, her mind shutting down, unable to reconcile the purity of his heartfelt confession with his sudden demand for her to leave.

Had he just confessed his love only to tell her he could no longer afford to have her near? She'd always thought his desire for his family name and heritage was the most important thing to him, that she'd end up losing him sooner rather than later. But after he'd told her she was everything to him, and she believed he meant it, what could his abrupt demand mean?

"Do you trust me?" His clipped question cut through her chaos.

She did, with her life, and now the life of their baby. Whether she'd ever be in his life again… That was what she didn't trust.

He repeated the question, more urgent and agitated, and she nodded weakly.

"Then trust me now. Trust that I love you, and that I'll do anything for your love. For *our* love and *our* child. Trust that without a single second of doubt…and leave. Now. Please."

The entreaty for an explanation congealed in her throat. She had to trust he had the best reason for jump-starting her heart, which had been smothered in despair, only to rip it out of her chest by tearing her from his side so abruptly.

She hung limp in his arms as he helped her to her feet, then fetched her stuff and fitted it over her shoulder.

"Steve is waiting outside. He'll be with you all

through. Take this phone. Call me the moment you board the plane."

Her hand trembled around the phone he'd pushed into it. Then he stood back, deprived her of his warmth and touch. She almost heaped to the ground without his support.

But he nodded for her, imploring her to go. Numb, she acquiesced, stumbled away from him to the open door, found most of her colleagues out of their offices, hanging in the corridor, openly watching. They must have witnessed the whole episode. And no doubt documented it, too. It might already be on the internet and trending on some social media site.

Uncaring what they did, or who saw this, feeling destroyed, even more than the first time she'd walked away from him, she turned to take what felt like her last look at him.

Raiden. Her only love.

He was looking back at her as if she'd taken his heart with her and was dragging it away from his body.

Though he'd made it sound as if she'd definitely see him again, that this was merely some emergency damage-control maneuver he had to execute, she felt this was the end.

Saying goodbye in her heart, because hope was more mutilating than despair, she turned and walked away from him.

Ten

Raiden watched Scarlett walk away unsteadily, passing through her colleagues, feeling as if his life force was draining out of his body with her every receding step.

Now that everyone realized this was for real, that he'd just sent her away, their yammering curiosity turned to vocal concern. Some strode by her side, anxiously asking if they could help, if she needed anything. The way she waved away their interest and offers of help told him she was barely holding herself upright and together. He wanted to roar for everyone to leave her alone, but had to stand there and suffer every heartbreaking second of her disappearance.

The moment he could no longer see her, he turned away, struggling with the tears that surged from his depths. He didn't want one of those people catching a photo of him in this condition. It might undermine all he was trying to do.

Getting his phone out, he called Steve, went over the details of the next few days. The specific bodyguards assigned to Scarlett's constant guard duty, the protocols they'd follow, the hourly reports they'd relay to him and everything else that ensured she'd have security no head of state ever had.

Afterward, he stood there, in the office that was no longer hers, waiting for Steve to take her away from him, struggling not to run out after her, come what may. Letting her go was the hardest test of his control ever.

But he had to do it. He had to make the Yakuza think he'd given her her marching orders. And he had to do it where people would witness it and run to make it public knowledge.

He didn't know how long it would be before the plan he'd concocted with his brothers worked, and worked perfectly. And the next two weeks, until the date of his supposed wedding, were the most dangerous time for Scarlett to remain here.

After the threat had been made, her continued presence, especially now that her pregnancy was a widespread scandal, would be considered a direct danger to the Yakuza's interests, and a flaunting of their displeasure. The Yakuza might consider both transgressions worthy of a disciplinary strike.

He'd hoped he could have only explained why he couldn't risk her staying even the night here. But all he'd been able to do was tell her how he felt, promise her forever, even as he begged her to leave. He'd hoped she'd believe him, in her heart at least, until he could explain more. And that her stunned confusion as she'd walked away would convince anyone this was an abrupt and permanent separation.

Now he'd wait until she was out of even his bodyguards' earshot to call her on the secure line he'd given her and explain. He was taking no chances she might be monitored now, since he couldn't be. He had to convince the Yakuza he had complied.

But he wouldn't fully explain the kind of danger he was protecting her from, couldn't bear causing her even more agitation. But at least, until he resolved this situation, she was safe.

Yet even he, with his unlimited resources, knew there was no way to keep her perfectly safe for more than a few days without imprisoning her, and alerting her stalkers to the fact that they were on to them. So those days would have to do. He and his brothers had a brief window of time to bring this to a permanent end.

Needing to put the last touch on this scene, he walked out. The office denizens flocked around him as they would a rock star, asking him questions as the paparazzi would.

Once outside, he finally acknowledged he wasn't walking alone, turned to them and gave the statement he knew would travel around Japan in minutes afterward.

Every lie cut him deeply, but he forced them out with what he hoped was a smile of nonchalance and not a grimace of agony.

"Regretfully, Ms. Delacroix won't be back. But she will continue her excellent work remotely until her projects are up and running. As for her pregnancy, it was a false alarm. And yes, my wedding is still in two weeks' time."

A dozen voices rose with a dozen questions, but this time he waved them away and entered the other limo waiting for him.

As they drove away, he put up the privacy barrier and sagged back into his seat, counting the minutes before he could call Scarlett again. After that, he'd begin counting the seconds until he could see her again.

And this time remain with her forever.

"This damned plan is taking *forever!*"

Raiden's vicious growl was followed by a minor crash.

He'd startled the flight attendant placing his meal in front of him out of her wits, making her drop the tray.

Gritting an apology and waving away her attempt to put things straight, he turned a blind gaze out of the window of his private jet, trying to rein back the constant boiling inside him. Not even the martial arts techniques he'd perfected had managed to bring him a measure of relaxation. He was spiraling out of control.

"It's been only two weeks." Numair's calm response through the phone line only poured fuel on his fire.

"That's temporally speaking," Raiden bit off.

"I wasn't aware there was another parameter we can measure time with."

"Phantom, attempting wit on me right now might cause me that stroke you all keep saying I'm trying to give myself." He paused for a second then almost shouted, "I don't care how long it's really been. It's been longer than my endurance."

"Your endurance lasted two seconds after she left."

He opened his mouth to blast him back with something, then closed it. For said endurance had been depleted *before* she'd left.

Numair was also right. Logically speaking, it hadn't been too long. Though the combined might of his brothers was mind-boggling, it couldn't have possibly taken them less than two weeks to untangle and reroute the web of interests, to tie all loose ends and to put all safety measures irrevocably in place.

But his brothers had already done that. It

wasn't until the wedding invitees had filled the ballroom hours ago that Numair and Richard had given the signal that all danger was over. Hashimoto had then walked in to announce the cancellation of the wedding. Raiden had followed his speech, apologizing for the last-second change of plans and assuring everyone dinner and entertainment were still on. Then he'd hurtled out of the hotel and onto his jet heading to New York. To Scarlett.

Then damn Numair had called him after take-off to tell him to come back, or at least not to go to Scarlett, and wait in New York until he told him he could see her. Numair claimed they weren't finished yet, and that he'd jumped the gun.

Numair insisted that they had yet to put on the finishing touch, what would have everyone willing to kill each other to keep Scarlett and their child safe.

Now everything inside him snapped. "Finish this, Numair. Kill whomever you have to kill and finish it. And don't say I have to wait again. I *can't*. And even if I can, I already called Scarlett

266   SCANDALOUSLY EXPECTING HIS CHILD

and told her I'm on my way. And I won't disappoint her again. I won't. *Do you hear me?*"

After his last bellowed words, total silence ensued on the other side.

Then he heard snickering. Snickering?

"I think the gods of Olympus heard you, Lightning."

"I didn't know you had it in you, Phantom."

Raiden frowned. That was Richard's voice, followed by Jakob's. What was going on here?

"We made a bet whether Phantom would have the heart to pull your strings, Lightning." That was Ivan.

"I bet against him, said he couldn't torture you a second more than you've already been tortured." Jakob groaned. "Now I have to submit to *his* torture for a whole day. He'll probably make me endure his company."

Rafael's apologetic voice came on. "I tried to stop them. But you know not even bullets can stop that herd."

"It's a send-off gift from all of us," Ivan teased. "For the way you've abused us all during the past two weeks."

"You tortured me most of all." Antonio yawned

loudly before continuing, "Calling me one minute for updates on my role in the plan, and the very next minute with obsessions about Scarlett's pregnancy. Do you know I slept on my feet during surgery today? And dreamed?"

Raiden shook his head, not really taking it all in. "You mean there's no finishing touch?"

A beat passed, then he heard more groans.

"He didn't even register that this was a prank," Jakob lamented.

"Good for you, Raiden." Rafael laughed. "You turned the tables on them without even meaning to."

"Should have known there was no pranking a love zombie," Ivan sniggered.

"God, that love malady is horrific." He could hear the disgusted shudder in Jakob's voice. "Bones, have you invented a vaccine for it yet? I'm willing to be your test subject."

"There *is* a finishing touch," Numair spoke up, ending his brothers' to and fro. "And it was put in place before we gave you the go-ahead earlier today. The Yakuza would now kill themselves and their families before they came near your wife and child."

After that, he could no longer hear anything. He didn't even know when the conversation came to an end.

All he knew was that he could finally be reunited with Scarlett. And that Numair had said *your wife and child*.

His wife and child.

Scarlett and their miracle.

His, at last. As he'd always be theirs.

Fifteen hours later, he stood on Scarlett's doorstep.

He'd spent hours of that time with her on the phone, telling her everything, now that it had all worked out. When he'd sent her away initially, he'd told her only that he was involved in a very delicate situation that he had to resolve with her out of the way. Finding out the details and magnitude of the averted danger had made her break down again.

She'd had frequent crises during the past two weeks. Though she no longer had any doubt that he was hers, she'd had so much terrible misfortune in her life, she believed something, anything, would happen, and prevent them from being together. No matter how he swore nothing would, the fear, their separation and pregnancy hormones played havoc with her moods and nerves.

Then she opened the door.

It felt as if his very heart, what had been ripped from his chest, stood across that threshold. The desolation of the time without him, the dread that fate would deal her another blow—this time a final one that wouldn't be survivable—lined her face, streaked her cheeks, hunched her body. She looked as terrible as he did. And like the most beautiful thing he'd ever seen. She was the one thing he wanted to see, to savor and wonder at for the rest of his life.

Then they were fused, straining to get closer, kissing, moaning, smiling, shedding tears, tearing clothes, pleading for more, for now, for everything, always everything.

Then she was in his arms, taken, contained; then he found himself on top of her on a bed and they were almost fighting each other for a faster descent into oblivion. Then finally they were merged, cresting then crashing into ecstasy.

Their union was brief, ferocious and earth-shattering, releasing all their pent-up dreads and longings.

A long time afterward, from the deepest well of satiation, he heard her voice, raw with her episodes of weeping, and just now with her abandon.

"I never wanted this."

He rose on his elbow, frowning down at her.

She elaborated. "I never wanted you to leave all your plans and dreams behind for me. With everything in me I hoped that you would reclaim your heritage and have a family, your family, again."

He smiled his adoration and indulgence down at her. "*You* are my family. And you're even giving me two family members at once. As for my heritage, I will have one. The one we'll make together and pass on to our child."

Her turbid eyes filled with the tears that now came so easily to her. "But there must have been a way to have both—your heritage and me. I would have been yours no matter what. I don't need legalities to make me yours."

"But I need to make you mine with legalities and with every other way there is or is still to be invented." When she grimaced and buried her face in his chest, he pulled her back. "I want you as my wife, and I want to be your husband. I always wanted that, from the first moment I saw you. And I continued to want you against all odds, all through the years." He suddenly huffed as a memory hit him. "Do you know that before I met you again and I thought I'd have to have heirs, I was resigned that I'd have to close my eyes and think of you so I could…perform?"

"God, Raiden, don't—"

"If you can't even stomach thinking of me in a hypothetical bed with a hypothetical woman—"

"Megumi wasn't so hypothetical."

He threw his head back on a delighted laugh at her growl. "See? You may think you could have shared me for the sake of my mission to reacquire my family name, but you're almost sick to your stomach just imagining it in retrospect, even when you know it will never happen."

"I would have stomached anything to be with you. At least, I would have lived with permanent nausea. I was a beggar who didn't dream she could be a chooser."

He crushed her to him, his eyes reproving.

"You were never a beggar. You were always my mistress, in all meanings of the word. Mistress of my heart, queen of my life. I was born to love you, too."

He received her surge as she flung herself at him, squeezed her tighter into himself. "I dreamed of reclaiming my heritage and my family because I thought I'd be able to fill the emptiness inside me with duty and tradition, that they'd be anchors to give my life purpose. Then I found you, and I no longer needed anything but you. I only searched for them again when I lost you, to fill the void your loss left behind. But you're back with me, and you're mine, have always been mine like I've always been yours. You fill my every emptiness—you are my anchor. You and the family we'll create together. You are my counterpart, the other half of my soul, the only one who's ever understood me, the darkness and pain and scars I have inside me, and also the power, resilience and indomitable will. We're the same, and we're the only ones to soothe and heal each other, and to give each other the endless love we need."

After dragging him down for a fierce, thankful kiss, she sank back, playing lovingly with his hair, her brilliant eyes glittering with tears and adoration. "When I wanted to do something that mattered, all I could think of was you, when you were a child, helpless and alone, and I wanted to help all the children who found themselves in your same situation."

His heart convulsed at yet another proof of her total love for him. "You suffered worse. Why didn't you direct your efforts toward girls who suffer the same as you did?"

"Because I love you more than I love myself. Way more." And he believed her. For he loved her way beyond how he loved himself or anything else. "Imagining your pain hurt me more than remembering experiencing my own. But once this shelter project is up and running, I'll do what you suggest, too, in my original region. But there, I won't be up against natural disasters, but organized crime." She sank kneading fingers in his arm. "I'll need your muscle there."

Body going rigid with arousal all over again, he groaned. "My every muscle is at your disposal. And my brothers', too."

She giggled. "Are you sure they'd be open to

SCANDALOUSLY EXPECTING HIS CHILD

that? Antonio called me when you were on your way and begged me to get you off his back. The poor man is entering chronic sleep deprivation because you're obsessing about my pregnancy."

"So what? That man can operate in his sleep. He actually did yesterday." She chuckled again, and he melted a caress down the delightful curve of her cheek. "So how do you feel about adoption?"

After a moment's surprise at his abrupt change of subject, she smiled widely. "I feel that now that I'm going to have a billionaire ninja husband, I'd like to adopt four children."

His eyebrows shot up. "Why four?"

"Because I have my eye on two girls and two boys in the shelter. And they have their eye on me. Ages two to six. I was thinking how I would be able to adopt them alone, but now…"

"We'll adopt them together. And our baby will be born to find she or he already has a huge family waiting to love her or him."

"Uh…why don't you think about it some more? Adoption is a huge decision, even bigger than deciding to have a biological child."

"I know that. And I've already thought. Why

do you think I asked you what you feel about it?" A consideration suddenly hit him. "Or did you only consider adoption when you thought you wouldn't have a child of your own?"

"Knowing I'll have a child of my own doesn't change a thing. I want to help as many children as I can, give them security, and if possible, a loving home."

"You're saving the child I was in them, aren't you?" When she nodded and buried her face in his chest, he lifted her chin, held her swimming eyes that glittered azure in the soft lights. "And we'll also save the child *you* were. An older girl who's been passed over for adoption from your part of the world."

She dived into his arms again with a smothered cry of poignancy...and the doorbell rang.

Frowning, he sat up. "Expecting someone?"

"I didn't even tell anyone I was back."

On alert in a split second, he sprang from the bed, making her whoop in delight at his elastic rebound.

"Wow," she breathed as she rushed to put on her dressing gown. "One day you must show me all the ninja stuff you can do."

"I showed you many so far." Then he showed her another trick, literally jumping into his pants.

As she jumped and clapped, he placed his fingers on his lips as he rushed soundlessly out of the bedroom.

She rushed after him. "Didn't you resolve everything with the Yakuza? Why are you alarmed now?"

He again gestured for her to lower her voice. "Because no one should be calling on you, now or at all."

"Aren't your bodyguards still around?"

"That's what's worrying me. That they didn't give us a heads-up and let someone come all the way to your door."

"Then they must have thought that someone would certainly be welcome."

"I'm not taking any chances."

She suddenly slapped her forehead. "You made me forget I have a video intercom."

He blinked at her. It seemed his circuits had been irrevocably fried, wiping out all his ingrained training. He'd have to train all over again. He'd have to reinstall simple logic.

Feeling sheepish, he followed her as she

checked the video feed. With a gun pointed at the door.

Then he saw who it was and his arms fell to his sides, the gun dangling loosely in one hand.

It was his uncle, Megumi and Hiro.

With a cry of surprise, Scarlett rushed to open the door.

Raiden stood frozen, unable to even come up with a reason that the unlikely trio was here. He'd thought he'd never see them again, let alone together.

He watched Scarlett welcome them inside, hugging Hiro, her face alight with pleasure at seeing her friend, and he could swear she was really pleased to see the other two, too.

The trio looked over at Raiden, their gazes drawn to the gun in his hand.

He waved it in self-deprecation. "I assume I don't need this and that you come in peace?"

Megumi giggled. Giggled! And such a merry sound, too.

Seemed it had been the prospect of marrying him that had been the reason for her stilted attitude.

As he put the gun away, Scarlett invited them all into her living room.

As soon as they sat down, Hiro blurted out, "I wouldn't have blamed you if you shot me on sight, Kuroshiro-san."

"When I thought you were interested in Scarlett, you were definitely in danger. Now, as her best friend, you've been drafted to the role of mine, too."

"It would be my honor to have you as a friend and ally, Kuroshiro-san." Hiro extended a hand to him, his eyes warm for the first time.

Raiden shook his hand. "If we're going to be friends, you'd better get used to calling me Raiden. And I'll call you like my lady calls you…Hiro." He slapped Hiro on the back and winked at his absolute surprise. "Next time you want to force me to do the right thing, just pick up the phone and threaten me. I'd rather be given the chance to avoid being smeared all over the tabloids and the World Wide Web." Hiro looked so mortified he took pity on him. "And if we're going to be friends and allies, we need to start working on your sense of humor. I was only teasing."

"You shouldn't be," Hiro objected. "I thought-lessly caused you and Scarlett, and at the time Hashimoto-sama and Megumi-san, a terrible scandal."

He grinned as he gathered Scarlett to his side. "From where I'm sitting, what you did was part of a sequence of events that led to me being here, the happiest man in existence."

Scarlett raised her hand. "Happiest woman in *history* here."

Though they'd just said the truth, she was clearly unable to bear seeing her friend beating himself up over this and she needed to make him exonerate himself. He felt the same way. Even if Hiro's actions could have caused untold damage, they hadn't. And what he and Scarlett had now was so unbelievable, he could forgive anyone anything.

"And then you were only defending your be-loved," Raiden added. "Saving her from a fate worse than death—marrying a man who loves another while she loves you." He grinned widely at Megumi, then at the still-chagrined man. "So that makes you a hero in my eyes."

"You might both forgive me in your magnanimity, because somehow my actions caused you only temporary distress. But that things were resolved so spectacularly was no thanks to me. So I reserve the right not to forgive myself, and to be forever at your disposal, should you require satisfaction."

"Just take that get-out-of-jail-free card, Hiro. I will no doubt need one from you at a future date." At Hiro's reluctant nod, with one last smile, Raiden turned his gaze to his uncle. "Not that I'm not thrilled for this unexpected opportunity to see you again, but I really thought I never would. So what brings you here? Whatever you needed, you know I'm forever at your disposal and I would come to you wherever you are."

"I had to be the one to come to you to make the offer," Hashimoto said.

"What offer?"

"When you terminated the marriage adoption, I felt disgraced and wanted to forever cut any ties with you. But then I remembered how I worried about you when you were under threat, and realized I already consider you family. The real disgrace would be to cling to pride and put

gossip and public censorship ahead of true re-
lationships."

Hashimoto suddenly leaned forward, took
Raiden's hand and Scarlett's, gathered them together and held them in both of his. "After all
the dust settled, I remembered when you said
how you'd wished we would have been family. I still feel the same way. I am here offering
you the name of our family, and the place at its
head—the same things you would have gotten
through the marriage adoption. But now I'm offering them through adoption alone."

Though that was yet another development in
a string of unexpected ones, the strange part
was what Raiden had been so passionate about
ten weeks ago didn't turn a hair in him now. He
truly had everything he wanted or needed as
long as he had Scarlett.

He shook his head. "This is no longer something I want or need. My family is right here."
He tightened his arm around Scarlett's shoulder.
She only looked up at him with eyes that were
at once stricken and admonishing.

"But this time we don't only want you, we
want to adopt you as a married couple," Hashi-

moto rushed to add. "And this is what our family hopes you would both consider—both of you taking our family name, making our family yours."

A long moment of silence followed his offer.

Then Raiden exhaled. "That's a very generous offer, Takeo-sama, but I still have to decline."

"But why, Raiden-san?" That was Megumi, at last breaking her usual silence. "We would have been catastrophic as spouses, but I just know it's because you were meant to be my brother. And I would love nothing more than to have Scarlett-san as my sister."

"And now Hashimoto-sama has agreed to give me Megumi-chan's hand in marriage," Hiro said eagerly. "I would no longer be only your friend, but your brother, too."

Delighted for both him and Megumi, Raiden clapped him on the back again. "You move fast, don't you, Hiro? Good for you." He turned to Megumi, who was blushing delicately. "You two feel to me as if you were once one whole that was split into two. It's so good seeing you becoming one again."

"So won't you reconsider?" Megumi asked, her eyes entreating. "Why are you refusing at all?"

He turned somber eyes to Hashimoto. "Because I haven't forgotten what you said about Scarlett, how you viewed her. Scarlett is and has always been the most upstanding and heroic person I know. I don't only worship her, but I respect and admire her more than anyone in the world. I would have nothing but the absolute best for her, and I would certainly never expose her to being considered an evil to be tolerated but secretly reviled, because your family still needs me."

Scarlett threaded her arm through his and looked up at him, her eyes silently scolding. "Mr. Hashimoto was under too much pressure at the time, not to mention misconceptions."

Hashimoto jumped on Scarlett's life raft. "That is true, and I now regret my words, and my thoughts. I had no proof to support them but hearsay, just because your presence went against my family's best interests. Can you possibly accept my apology and my assurances that my opinion was one of ignorance and self-service, but one that I have irrevocably changed?"

"Of *course* I accept, Mr. Hashimoto," Scarlett said fervently. "I almost caused you all huge losses, just being there, just loving Raiden. And like Hiro said, it's no thanks to me that everything has been averted and we've reached this happy moment." As Raiden began to protest, she turned to him and hugged him around the waist, all her love in her eyes. "Let's not dwell on anything that happened before today. The past is dead and gone. Let's only remember the good parts of it, and look forward to a magnificent future."

He knew what she meant. They might never be able to forget the past, but it had led them to this point, where they were unimaginably blessed by having each other.

She brought him down to her for a fierce, brief kiss. "But we both do need a family, to make up for the ones we lost. And it will be the best thing for our coming baby, and any other children we will have, to have a big family to dote on them."

Suddenly unable to wait a second longer, he swept her in his arms, heaved up to his feet and strode back to her bedroom.

At her squeaking protest, he stopped, looked

back at the trio, found them on their feet, look-ing crestfallen.

He raised a mocking eyebrow at them. "Uh, sorry, were you waiting for a response from me?" He groaned in pleasure as Scarlett gave his jaw a punishing nip. His eyes laughed down at her, then back at the guests. "Let me give you a tip for future reference. Once Scarlett has spo-ken, I am but the executor of her will. She wants us to be family, we *will* be family."

After a moment's uncertainty, the trio's faces split with smiles, then they each advanced on them, all delighted relief.

At Scarlett's loving nudge, he put her back on her feet so she could receive with him the hugs of the three people who would be their family.

After an interlude of mutual thanks and excite-ment, especially on the side of the ladies, who seemed to be delighted to have a girlfriend in their testosterone-dominated lives, Raiden swept Scarlett back up into his arms.

This time their guests took the hint and rushed to the door. Scarlett spluttered that he put her down, that they should stay longer, that she hadn't even offered them something to drink.

But this time he didn't heed her, and the trio insisted on leaving. It was time, Hashimoto said, to leave the two of them to continue their reunion after such a harrowing separation.

Raiden called after them when they were at the door, "I *am* grateful we will be family. But remember, we will only be because Scarlett decreed it. Now you all owe her."

Their voices rose in corroboration as they closed the door behind them. Then he raced with her to her bedroom.

Putting her down on the still-rumpled sheets, as if he was laying down his heart, he pulled off his clothes, then hers, and came down into her arms.

"I wasn't just making him squirm, you know," he said against her lips. "I was going to insist on refusing."

She flushed with passion and embarrassment, unable as usual to take her dues. "But you didn't, and now you'll have everything you ever dreamed of and deserve. I won't have to feel perpetually sad and guilty that my presence in your life deprived you of such a huge thing."

"It will be huge only because I will share it

with you. But if not for you, for your forgiveness and your desire to be part of a family, I wouldn't have accepted. So they do owe you. Just as I owe you my happiness, my very life."

Crying out, she pulled him down to her. "And I owe you mine."

And she took him inside her, taking him home, his one and only home, forever.

* * * * *

MILLS & BOON®

Why shop at millsandboon.co.uk?

Each year, thousands of romance readers find their perfect read at millsandboon.co.uk. That's because we're passionate about bringing you the very best romantic fiction. Here are some of the advantages of shopping at www.millsandboon.co.uk:

* **Get new books first**—you'll be able to buy your favourite books one month before they hit the shops

* **Get exclusive discounts**—you'll also be able to buy our specially created monthly collections, with up to 50% off the RRP

* **Find your favourite authors**—latest news, interviews and new releases for all your favourite authors and series on our website, plus ideas for what to try next

* **Join in**—once you've bought your favourite books, don't forget to register with us to rate, review and join in the discussions

Visit **www.millsandboon.co.uk**
for all this and more today!

MILLS_WEB_LP